Timeless
an Anthology

Edited By
Denise Vitola

All rights reserved. No part of this publication may be reproduced or transmitted in any form or by any means, electronic or mechanical, including photocopy, recording, or any information storage and retrieval system, without the prior written permission of the publisher, except in the case of brief quotations for reviews. No part of this book may be scanned, uploaded or distributed via the Internet, without the publisher's permission and is a violation of International copyright law and subjects the violator to severe fines and/or imprisonment.

Timeless
Copyright © 2012 by Cool Well Press, Inc.
ISBN: 978-1-61877-087-5
Editor – Denise Vitola
Cover Artist - DarkAshe Graphics

This book is a work of fiction. The names, characters, places, and incidents are products of the writer's imagination or have been used fictitiously and are not to be construed as real. Any resemblance to persons, living or dead, actual events, locale or organizations is entirely coincidental. The publisher does not have any control over and does not assume any responsibility for author or third-party Web sites or their content.

Published in the United States of America
First print edition: February 2012 Cool Well Press, Inc.
www.coolwellpress.com

Valentine's Day was first celebrated in 496 A.D., in remembrance of the martyrs who opposed Ancient Rome. They were known as Martyr Valentinus, which in Latin means those who are worthy, powerful, and strong. Over the centuries, Valentine's Day has come to represent a time when intimate companions show their love and affection. It also serves to remind us of love that has been lost.

And as far back as the misty ages go, men have always believed that there are immortals roaming the Earth. These immortals come in many forms, such as vampires, werewolves, shape-shifters, angels, and faery. Because these creatures are supernaturally strong and powerful, they might be referred to as the true Valentinus. They experience profound love and loss. While many are not worthy of this title, there are those whose love and sacrifice have made them exceptional role models. The stories that follow are about a few of these extraordinary beings.

Timeless: an Anthology

The Last Penny—5

Eternally Be Mine, Valentinus—43

The Gate of Ethos—63

The Boy and the Nymph—95

The Trippet Stones—113

The Waters of Life—149

The Sun and the Star—179

The Soul Gardener—199

The Scratcher—227

Author Bios—242

The Last Penny

Morgan Ashe

The Last Penny

3 pennies to go...

"I'm telling you. Stop giving that dog chocolate. What's the matter with you? You're just feeding his habit and teaching him bad habits."

The girl sounded exasperated to Alison. She shifted on the slate outcropping, waiting for the visitors to come into view. They were a few meters out but getting closer. The rock felt warm from the day's sun shining on it, a contrast to the cool evening air but not as warm as the water where her feet were submerged to the ankles. She crinkled her toes a little, scattering the tiny fish swimming in the spring's waters. Their small, darting bodies barely caused a ripple on the surface.

"Do you want to be the one to cut off his candy bar supply? Remember the *Outdoor Chocolatier's Demonstration Incident* last week? You're the one he sleeps with. Do you want to wake up with his face staring into yours?" the man said in a deep voice.

"What are you talking about? He does that already. Every time he wants something, in fact. He has no issue with bowling me over and standing on me until I give him what he wants."

"You have a point. Still, he's a hellhound, not a dog. Let him have it. It's not hurting him."

"Fine. Here, you lil sneak, enjoy it. It's my last one." The crinkly sound of a wrapper filled the night.

"You love him, stop complaining," the man said.

"Hush. Did you really have to say that out loud? You want him more spoiled than he already is? But, yes, he is kind of growing on me."

Their friendly banter made Alison smile. They sounded fun, but what was a hellhound, she wondered. A movement caught her eye and she turned to watch Cassia swim past, her long, wet hair sleeked back against her head. She moved quietly and then disappeared under the long branches of the weeping willow that draped into the spring's waters. The oceanid was careful never to be seen when people were around. Unlike Alison, she was not hidden from their gaze, not invisible to curious onlookers. Alison chewed her lower lip, worried about her friend. She didn't know what she could do for her.

Poor Cassia, even this beautiful evening probably failed to bring her comfort. And it was a beautiful evening. A full moon cast its reflected light on the glade and the spring's waters sparkled and danced in tune with the slight breeze. Cicadas hummed in every direction, the sound waxing and waning like a living entity, growing silent as the voices rose and louder during their lull. She lifted her face to the ebony sky and breathed in the sweet smell of the night, lush with the fragrance of summer's grasses and flowers.

The sound of voices interrupted her appreciation of the nightfall. "Tell me why we're out here again in the middle of nowhere at four a.m. when I should be getting some sleep? I have a test tomorrow, well today, in chemistry. It's mid-terms at last, and I need to go shopping for the prom. I can't believe I said I'd go with you."

"Beka, the prom experience is something not to be missed. I can't believe you weren't going. You need a well rounded life to balance your...er...extracurricular activities. I'll bet you've never sat on the beach and just watched the flames from a campfire while telling scary tales either."

"You mean raging ex-goddesses, hellhounds, and Friday evenings watching movies with my great uncle Jasper the Ghost aren't enough? Oh, and the occasional four a.m. stroll with a guy I only know as Death? Are you suggesting I need puppies and rainbows and proms, too? What's next, getting excited about a new pair of shoes?"

"You have two months before the prom. Stop obsessing. Why can't—?"

"Smokie!" the girl interrupted the man. "Get out of that water, you idiot. You remember what happened last week when I tried to give you a bath. You created so much steam it rained in my bathroom."

Noisy splashing and, strangely, what sounded like hissing to Alison replaced the voices.

A large gray, soaking wet—oh-my-God-that-can't-be-a-dog-it's-the-size-of-a-barn—animal leapt up on the rock with Alison and stared down at her with red glowing eyes. Wisps of smoke drifted from his nostrils and more tendrils curled from his fur. He gave a quick shake and sent droplets of water through the air. Each one stood out separately, almost frozen in time for a moment, glistening with the moon's light. Then a wet, hot nose pressed into Alison's face and the beast—Smokie, she surmised—began licking her cheek. "Eww," she said, holding out a hand to push him away. One final lick and he was gone, splashing back to the other side of the spring and the couple who were almost at its edge.

"Smokie... Don't. You. Dare. Stop," the man warned, but it was too late. Just as he had to her, the hellhound shook and rained water droplets over both the man and the woman. Beka shrieked and jumped back, avoiding most of it, but the man looked as if he'd just stepped out of a shower.

Alison watched as Beka giggled and then squealed as the man—Death? And just what kind of a name was that anyway—whirled around and caught her close to him. "There, now you can get as wet as I am," he taunted. She pulled away from him with another laugh and walked to the edge of the spring where Smokie was drinking vast quantities of water.

"So what is this place? It's lovely, but I don't see why we're here," she said.

"It's a wishing spring. I wanted you to see it under a full moon and make a wish. Throw in a coin." Death walked over to stand behind her.

Beka dug into a pocket of her jeans and pulled out something. Alison leaned forward expectantly, hoping it was a penny. It was. She watched the girl close her eyes and then toss the penny into the air. A small splash signaled its entry into the water and, inside Alison, one more rope chaining her to the spring loosened. *"Two more to go,"* that voice inside her head whispered. Hope grew. One day her curse would be finished, and she would be free of the confines of the spring. She looked over her shoulder toward the weeping willow. It wasn't going to be as easy for Cassia and not knowing how to help her made Alison sad. An aggravated voice had her turn back to the action on the other side.

"Smokie! Get off me, you furry, wet ape. This is not what I wished for. Who wants to kiss a hellhound? Gross, hellhound spit. Yuck."

"Oh?" Death leaned over and pushed Smokie off Beka. "Were you hoping for a kiss from someone else?"

"You know I can't tell you what I wished for, silly, or it won't come true."

Alison watched. The scene seemed to stand still in time for her for a second with Death leaning over Beka as she gazed up at him. Alison gave a long sigh at the romantic scene. Slowly, Death reached out and took both of Beka's hands in his and drew her up so she was standing next to him.

He is quite dashing, Alison thought, *with his dark hair tied back and a five o'clock shadow outlining his strong jaw.* He looked like a movie actor Alison had seen once in an old-fashioned Hollywood magazine. She turned her attention to Beka. She was…short. Somehow with her voice, Alison had expected someone taller, but Beka was…short. Smokie stood next to the couple and while he only reached to Death's waist, he stood almost as tall as Beka's chest. She was the girl-next-door cute and slender with long, dark wavy hair half way down her back. She was clad in faded jeans and a white, man's button-down shirt. Alison drew in her breath when she saw the boots though. They looked like leather and had an array of buckles and straps along the shaft that ran up to mid calf. It had been years since she could wear boots. Sometimes, she thought, the lack of a shopping spree was the hardest part to bear about her curse. Heck, she'd even settle for window-shopping at this point.

"*Girl,*" the voice inside her head said, *"do you have any idea how many times you have thought about shoes over the past twe—"*

"*Hush,*" she interrupted. *"Never stand between a girl and a pair of shoes."* The chuckle echoed a bit through her head, but there were no further comments. *For now*, she thought.

The couple hadn't moved. They were too busy looking at each other. *Yeesh, kiss her*, Alison thought. *Kiss her.* Death towered over Beka's slim form, and then he bent his head and kissed her. Alison breathed a sigh of relief.

Death and Beka broke apart and he wrapped his arms around her, holding her tight against him. Alison felt like a peeping Tom, but really there was so little to do around here and it was nice to see two people who fit together so well.

She sat daydreaming a little—or was it moondreaming? She giggled to herself. The hope inside her felt warm and happy, and she basked in that feeling for a moment. Maybe someday she'd find someone like Beka seemed to have. A yip from Smokie drew her out of her reverie. She opened her eyes to find herself looking across the pond and straight into Death's gaze. He still held Beka close, but now his head was raised and he was staring at…her. Looking at…her. No one had been able to look at her for almost twenty years. How was that possible? Alison drew in a deep breath. Wait. The hellhound. Smokie. He had seen her as well and had touched her. A wink from Death held her spellbound.

"Two more to go," he said loud enough for her to hear. "And, it will be soon. Then you have a little job to do for Thomas." Alison didn't know what he was talking about, but somewhere inside herself she knew he was right and there was a job she had to do when she was free. She nodded.

"What are you talking about? Who are you talking to?" Beka asked, pulling her arms from around Death's neck and stepping back.

"Nothing to worry about. Just a message I wanted to pass on. Thomas needed me to deliver that message to someone."

"You are not his messenger boy. Why didn't he deliver it?"

"He had an emergency. Someone had a deadline crisis and needed assistance. You know he's a writer's muse when he's not bedeviling Michael. Plus, he needed one more penny. Seemed he miscounted visitors. Silly angel never was very good at math. Come on. Let's go to the Shadow Street Diner. I'm in the mood for the world's best pancakes."

At the word pancakes, some serious woofing came from the underbrush and Alison could hear Smokie crashing his way back.

Alison heard Beka giggle. With a last glance and a nod at Alison, Death threaded his fingers through Beka's, and they began to walk down the path. Smokie bolted out from the shrubs and onto the path. He stopped for a second and looked toward Alison, his red eyes glowing in the shadows. A soft *chuff* and he was gone.

"Silly angel, my as—" the voice inside her sounded indignant before he cut himself off and fell silent, leaving Alison to ponder for a moment just who that voice belonged to. She shrugged and looked over at the willow. There was no noise, not even a ripple from beneath its lacey boughs. She lowered herself into the water and swam to join Cassia. It was dark, but enough light filtered in through the branches to let Alison see Cassia's

hunched body on the bank. The oceanid had her face buried in her hands and her slight body shook as sobs wracked her body. Alison swam quickly to her side and pulled herself out of the water to sit next to Cassia. Alison wrapped her arms around the oceanid and held her gently, making soothing noises.

"We'll figure something out, Cassia. I promise I won't stop until I can help you, too. There has to be a way out of your situation. We'll find it."

Soft hiccupping sounds escaped from Cassia. She seemed to be trying to control her tears but not doing a good job of it from Alison's perspective. And who could blame her? Alison's curse was only a few decades old—Cassia's was almost a thousand years. Tears stung Alison's eyes when she thought of how lonely and hopeless Cassia must have felt year after year of being tied to this spring, waiting for her one true love to find her and knowing he never could.

She remembered the look in Cassia's eyes when she had finally told Alison her story. That look of utter despair. What had been sadder was the love that had still shone, regardless of what a twit her love had been. Going off to rescue some silly dragon. Then disappearing, probably eaten up by the very dragon he had gone to save. Alison wished she could go punch him for Cassia, but that wasn't an option. He was long gone, and Cassia's curse had no chance of being lifted.

"You've been so good to me, Alison," Cassia whispered. "I don't know why you ever forgave me for what I did to you. I only hope someone can help you soon."

"*Shhh*, Cass, it's okay. I'm glad it happened, honestly. It's given me a chance to appreciate things fully. Stop upsetting yourself." Alison hugged Cassia tight, and together they rocked back and forth until the moon began to set and the sun's rays began to paint the sky a faint yellow.

Alison drew Cassia to her feet, and they walked over to the small cave they called home. After tucking Cassia into her bed of soft leaves and grasses, she went to her own little nest and fell into an exhausted sleep. But the dreams came…

Twenty years ago…

"Here it is. See I told you. Look at all those coins. We can take enough to go to the movies and even get some popcorn." Emma's shrill voice caused Alison to wince. She looked at the spring and saw coins sitting on the silt under the clear waters. There must have been hundreds. Far from being tempted to gather them like her sister, she wanted them to stay. Each coin represented a wish from its thrower—a hope, a dream. They weren't there for movie tickets or popcorn. Emma was now up to her knees in the water, bending over time and again to gather more and more coins.

"Stop it, Emma. That money isn't yours. It belongs to the spring. You shouldn't take them. Come on, we'll ask Mom for a few dollars. That's all we need. This summer after graduation, we can get jobs and go see all the movies we want." Alison reached over, grabbed her sister's arm, and tried to guide her toward the bank. Emma angrily pulled her arm away and bent again.

Out of the corner of her eye, Alison caught a shadow and turned to look. Her eyes widened at what she saw. Treading water in the middle of the spring was a young lady. Long black hair trailed behind her and her penetrating blue gaze was fixed on Emma and Alison. The expression on her face was far from friendly or welcoming.

"Um…Emma, get out now. Look. Look over there. Someone is watching us."

Emma didn't look, instead concentrating on stuffing more and more coins in her pockets. "Just shut up, you brat, and help me. I've done this before, and no one has ever been here. It's in the middle of nowhere."

"You've stolen the coins from here before?" Alison was sad, and she stopped worrying about the woman in the spring for a moment. This wasn't how their mother had raised them. Their father had died in a car accident years before, and their mom was barely able to support them on her salary from the grocery store, but she always had taught them that earning what they needed was the only way.

"It's not stealing. It's no one's money, and I need it more than the water does."

"Actually, girl, it's my money, and you are taking what is mine." The low-pitched voice grew louder as the woman swam behind Emma.

Emma twirled, her mouth agape as she realized there really was someone watching them.

Now *she believes me*, Alison thought.

"Wh-who are you?" Emma stuttered. Alison had never seen her at a loss for words before. Usually Emma brazened it out in bad situations, and boy oh boy had there been situations. Too many for Alison to count, but never one this serious…or strange.

"I am the guardian of this spring, and you are taking away wishes and dreams. Wishes and dreams that have no hope of ever coming true, now. Put them down and leave. Never come back here." The woman's eyes grew stormier with each word, and Alison could swear she felt her hair starting to stand on end as tingles raced along her skin. She shivered in growing fear and grabbed Emma's arm again, tugging and pulling it.

"That's stupid," Emma said. "These are just coins. Coins here for the taking. They belong to no one, not you, not the spring. They're mine." She ran the flat of her free hand along the surface of the water, sending a spray of water at the woman. "Go away and leave me alone."

Alison's tugging on Emma's arm finally had some effect, and Emma went off balance. She had to grab onto Alison for support to stop from falling.

"You think you are so smart, little girl? I don't think so. I think you need to learn a lesson. Listen to my words. You are destined to remain at the spring with me to understand the error of your ways. You will stay until a hundred dollars in pennies have been thrown into the waters and a wish is made for you." The guardian reached up to grab Emma, but she stepped back and pushed Alison into the guardian's grasp.

"No." Both Alison and the guardian cried out at the same time, but it was too late. Like a rope being drawn tight, Alison felt the weight of the enchantment wrap around her body and what sounded like a lightning bolt sizzled through the air. *"It is done,"* a voice whispered in her head.

Emma splashed her way to the bank and stood there, her eyes wild and scared. Then, suddenly, she started to laugh. She pointed at Alison who stood there frozen, still held by the guardian.

"Look at the two of you. You both deserve each other. Stick-in-the-mud goody-two-shoes. No one helps anyone. You have to help yourself. I'm going to the movies, and I'm getting lots of popcorn." She jingled the coins in her pocket and ran down the path.

"Nooooo. Emma, don't leave me here. Please, come back." Alison pulled herself out of the guardian's arms and following Emma's example splashed her way to the edge. She climbed to the bank and started to follow Emma, but something stopped her. It was like she slammed into an invisible wall. She couldn't go any further.

She looked over her shoulder and saw the guardian treading water, a sad look on her face. "I'm sorry," the woman said. "It was supposed to be her, not you. But when I touched you, the curse fell on you. I'm so sorry."

Alison fell to her knees on the soft grassy bank and began to weep. She heard the woman say something above her, but a voice in her head spoke, *"One thousand pennies to go."* She moaned as the roaring in her ears increased until everything was drowned out. The tears didn't stop even when she felt the woman's arms enfold her, and she was held tight.

Present day...

"Alison. Alison, wake up. It's just a dream, honey. It's just a dream."

Alison woke to the dim glow lighting up the little cave, and Cassia's concerned face.

"I'm okay, Cassia. I'm okay." Alison sat up and wrapped her arms around her drawn up knees. "Somehow, someday, we're both going to be free. I can't believe there is nothing to free you."

"There isn't, honey. You know my chance of freedom disappeared when my love died. I will be tied to this spring forever or until it dries up and I fade with it."

"Cassia, I remembered something. When you came up to me on the bank that first day, you said something. What did you say?"

Alison saw a flicker of a smile cross Cassia's face. "I wished your sister a very long life full of youth. I could think of no other wish for one such as she."

"How is that bad?" Alison questioned.

"Your sister probably would not think so either, but I am a believer of circles. You've probably heard it as you reap what you sow. I wanted to make sure she had the opportunity to reap what she'd sown."

Alison thought about that for a moment then looked at Cassia and laughed. For the first time in a long time, Cassia laughed back.

2 pennies to go…

"Kay, slow down a little bit. I think I see something on this side path. Let's go this way instead."

"Sounds good, darling. Let's try it. We've never been the-road-most-travelled type."

Alison peeked out from the reeds. A tall woman with long black hair stood at the edge of the waters, her hand clasped firmly in the hand of an even taller man. He was handsome in a rugged manner. His dark hair was clipped close to his head, and he had an equally close-cropped mustache and beard. They stood shoulder to shoulder looking at the small waterfall that flowed on the one side.

"Oh, Dale, look it's a spring. How pretty that is with the water trickling down the rocks. I've never seen water so clear. I keep expecting a water sprite or spirit to pop her head up and wave. It looks like something right out of mythology or a fairy tale, doesn't it?"

"It does, doesn't it? I wonder who the guardian of this one is? Someone very lonely, I'd imagine. This is certainly off the beaten path."

"You might be right. The sound of the water makes me think of someone crying."

"Aww, honey, look. There are coins at the bottom. It's a wishing spring. Do you remember what your parents had us do before we got married?" Dale wrapped his arm around Kay's shoulders and hugged her tight to his side

"Yeah. Saving a thousand dollars in pennies took us forever, especially since we couldn't go to the bank and turn in our other change. I thought it would take a lifetime to save that many."

"Looking back I think it was smart of them. It gave us time to learn about each other rather than rush into marriage and be sorry. So many years ago... Look where we are now. Hey, do you have our special penny with you?"

Alison saw the lady put a hand up and cover the pocket of her jeans. "In here. Why?"

"Do you realize what today is? Today is the anniversary of the day we collected the last penny. The very penny you've kept."

Kay laughed and cupped her free hand around Dale's face. She stood on her tiptoes and gave him a kiss on the lips. "You're the only man I know who remembers dates. Here it is." Kay reached into her pocket and pulled out a coin. She handed it to Dale.

"I think it's fate we found a wishing spring on the anniversary of the day we collected that penny. I think we should make a wish with it. It will be our special wish."

"Do we wish together or separately? I don't know if it works if we both know what the wish is."

"It will. We do it together. Together, like we've done everything else. What do you want to wish for?"

"Something for Bryan? Wealth, fame, power, good luck, or something like that?"

"Aww, honey, we don't have to wish for any of that. Our son will do well for himself. No...I have an idea, but I don't know why it just popped into my head. I hope you don't think it's strange. I think we should wish that those who guard the spring find happiness. Spread ours around so to speak."

"That's perfect, darling. Okay on the count of three throw it in."

"One, two, three."

Kerplunk.

Once again it seemed one more rope chaining Alison to the spring loosened. *"One more to go,"* that same little voice she always heard whispered. She was so happy, she squealed, and then clapped her hand over her mouth before she remembered the couple couldn't see or hear her.

"Dale, did you hear that noise? That didn't sound like any woodland animal I know."

"Who knows, honey, maybe they have unique squirrels around here or something. Come on, let's go get some ice cream or I hear there is a place that makes the world's best pancakes over on that strange little street. Shadow Street I believe it's called. How do pancakes sound?"

"Simply perfect."

They clasped hands again and wandered back up the trail.

Alison heard someone behind her and turned. Cassia stood there with a half smile on her face. "Looks like only one to go, Alison. I hope everything works out well. I'm sure it will."

"What do you mean? It's just one more penny and I'm free, right?"

"Well…it's not quite that simple. The person who throws it in has to make a wish for you—and there's a catch, they can't be told to wish for you."

"What? But how is that going to work? And…and what if it doesn't happen? What happens next? The possibility of that happening must be close to impossible." Alison could almost feel her heart sink to her feet as despair washed over her.

"Then it starts all over again. Don't worry, Alison. Something tells me it's going to work out. Just wait and see." Cassia patted Alison's shoulder and turned and left her standing in the reeds, too stunned to say a word.

One more penny...

"Let it go, Emma. I'm tired of talking about it with you. I've wanted to see what this path leads to for a long time now and you keep stopping me. What's going on? I told you a month ago we were through. You just don't get it. We have nothing in common and I want you to stop following me and showing up wherever I go. What do I need to do to make you understand that?" The young man's voice was tight with anger and his low baritone had no problem reaching Alison's ears. At the sound of the next voice, she sat up straight in shock. *No, it can't be*, she thought. *Not after all these years.*

"I don't want to walk down that way, Deacon. There are too many tangles and thorns. Let's go back and follow the other path. It's cleaner and my heels won't get caught in the stones. Besides, I want to talk to you about everything. I miss you." The voice was shrill and petulant.

It's Emma, Alison thought. *It's really her.*

"Stop, Deacon. I swear I won't go one more step."

"Fine, go back. I didn't want you following me anyway."

"Fine yourself. There is nothing down there but a stupid old spring. Have fun. I'm going to go find my fun somewhere else."

"How does she know there is a spring down here?" Alison heard him ask out loud as he approached the bank. "Why am I even wondering? Good riddance."

Alison's anticipation grew as Deacon got closer. His deep voice did something inside her that no one else's ever had. It actually felt like little fish were inside her tummy swimming around and bumping into each other. When he stepped into view, she gasped. He was dreamy.

"Dreamy?" the voice asked. *"No one uses that word anymore. You're supposed to use something like hunk or hot or handso—"*

"Did you swallow a thesaurus that only had words that start with H?" she interrupted. *"Don't you have something better to do?"*

"Not really. I'm rather enjoying the show, or rather, the preview."

"Huh?"

"Never mind."

Alison stopped listening to her inner visitor and watched as Deacon sat on the grass. He stared at the rocks and the waterfall for a while before lying back, gazing at the sky. Alison looked up and saw the puffy white clouds chasing each other. They blocked the sun over and over again, racing their shadows across the ground. She watched as his eyes kept closing for longer and longer periods of time until he slept.

Alison couldn't help herself. She finally swam to the bank, careful not to make a sound. She stood and waded out to the grass, tippy toeing over to simply stare down at him. There was something about Deacon that drew her. She didn't know what, but she had never felt like this before—excited, anxious, sad—all the emotions rolled over and through her like the clouds above.

She sat next to him, knowing that even if he woke, he couldn't see her. His lashes lay long and thick against his skin.

Why do men always have the nicest eyelashes, she thought. *It's totally unfair.*

"Here we go again," the voice said, sounding resigned. *"Can't we talk about something else?"*

"I really can't discuss current events, you know." Alison sighed. *"It's been awhile since that newspaper page blew in here and even then that was just the classifieds."*

She continued to gaze at Deacon, memorizing his details, wanting to keep his image in her thoughts to keep safe. Not for the first time, she despaired her fate, but for this one moment in time, he was hers.

"Young love is so painful to watch," the voice whispered in her head. *"I remember a long time ago there was this other water nymph who fell in love with someone who just watched himself in the water. He fell in love with his own reflection and had no time for her. That one didn't turn out very well."*

"You're talking about Echo and Narcissus?" Alison asked. *"Just how old are you? You must be ancie—"*

"Enough of that. Age is only a number you know. After all you are over thir—"

"Look at that squirrel," Alison interrupted the voice. *"Isn't he just adorable?"*

"Yes, let's change the subject. For now. I'll be back. I have to run a short errand." A chuckle went through her head and then the voice went silent.

"And stay away," she muttered.

The next few hours passed quickly. Alison sat guard over Deacon, from what she didn't know, but it made her feel needed chasing away a few curious spiders. While she couldn't interact with them like Cassie could she could send little bursts of static electricity towards them and change their direction. Deacon slept on, and she hoped she had a little more time with him before he woke and left.

"I'm back. Did you miss me?

"Um...no, not really. Don't you have more errands you could run for a while?"

"You shouldn't just sit here gawking, girl. You know I haven't heard you sing for a while. Why don't you sing something?"

"Last time I sang you said I was off-key and to stop the caterwauling."

"Sing something pretty. I'm in a mood."

Alison sighed. *"Okay."*

Alison looked at Deacon. She knew immediately which song she would sing for him. She'd heard it enough times from Cassia when she was mourning the loss of her love. Cassia's songs were not like what Alison had known. The song made her think of knights and unicorns and fairy tales. She began to sing in her soft contralto.

> I once was in a distant land
> And far away at that same time
> In a place so different yet
> You stood and watched the suns shine down
> And wondered even then
>
> Through space and time

Through fate or chance or even destiny
A day arose when stars aligned
And separate pieces met

I stood beside the fields of grass
Within a forest green
I turned to look and there beheld
My true love on the path

All through the light and shadows dark,
We'll keep our love so true
We'll walk the paths that life brings
And smell the wildflowers.

The sun shines brighter now
The stars burn hotter too
For everyday feels like the first
For now there is a we.

    Deacon felt himself gradually awaken to the soft tones of someone singing a haunting melody. He stayed still and didn't open his eyes. *She must be sitting right next to me*, he thought. *It's lovely, but how strange.* It was like an old-fashioned song that made him think of tales of Camelot, dragons, and Arthur. When the singer paused, he opened his eyes and looked. No one was there but the song's words continued to ring through his head for a moment.

"Who is there? Where are you?" he asked. "I can hear you. Come out and show yourself."

His ears were met with dead silence—even the crickets stopped their humming.

"Please, I didn't mean to be so abrupt," he pleaded as he sat up. "Your song is lovely. I want to hear it again." He heard a slight rustle to his side and turned to look, but nothing was there.

"Y-you can hear me?" a girl's voice whispered. "Y-you can really hear me?"

"Where are you? I can't see you," he replied.

"I'm right here, next to you. No one has been able to hear me for years. I don't understand why…"

"Who are you? What…are you?" Deacon wondered for a moment if he was dreaming, but the warm breeze on his face and the furtive rustling in the underbrush proved he wasn't.

"My name is Alison. I'm a…well…I'm one of the guardians of this spring."

For the next few hours they talked. Deacon wanted to learn everything about her, her likes, her dislikes. She seemed to soak up all the latest news about what had happened in the world since she'd been tied to the spring. In turn, he told her about himself, his travels, his studies.

As dusk drew near, he knew something special was happening between them. He wondered how this could work—if it could work—but for this moment he didn't care. All that was important was to talk to Alison, hear her voice, be close to her. Tomorrow would take care of itself. Still he had to try and find out more.

"How can you leave this spring? Is there a way the curse can be broken?" he asked.

"There are several things that must happen, but I can't talk about them. They will either happen or not. It's not up to me."

"What do we do until then? I want to talk to you again. I'll come back, but truthfully I don't want to leave."

"It's okay," Alison whispered. "I'll still be here tomorrow and the day after that and the day aft—"

"Shh, trust me, Alison. I'll be back. I promise."

A few more parting words and Deacon left.

Alison watched him. He never looked back but walked steadfastly down the path until he disappeared in the growing gloom of night. She stifled a sob. He was gone. It had been the most perfect afternoon ever but now would she ever see him again? She could only pray he would return. That night, she tossed and turned, dozing but never falling into a deep sleep. She was up and out of the cave's entrance at first light going to the bank and finding a soft spot she could sit and wait—a spot that was the closest she could get to the barrier to see Deacon take that first turn around the bend in the path.

Hours passed and still no sign of Deacon. Cassia swam over several times, her face troubled. Alison waved her off each time. She didn't want to talk, not to Cassie and not to the aggravating visitor in her head who had thankfully remained silent today thus far.

The midday sun burned down upon her when she finally gave up. She stood and walked to the water's edge.

*...We'll walk the paths that life brings
And smell the wildflowers.*

The sun shines brighter now—

She squealed in joy, interrupting the singer. *"Ouch, girl,"* her inner visitor's voice held a wince, but she ignored it. All she cared about was getting to the barrier to see Deacon.

"You came back."

"I'm sorry, Alison. I wanted to be here sooner, but I had a flat tire and for some reason my spare was flat, too. I didn't mean to worry you. I'm here now. And this is the only place I want to be. I thought about our talk all night and couldn't wait to get here."

She moved as close to him as she could, and, for the moment it was enough.

Every day during the next week, Alison woke at first light and hurried to get ready. She spent hours combing her hair, checking her reflection in the spring, straightening and smoothing out her only dress. *Spring nymphs have the ugliest dresses*, she grumped to herself. Why couldn't they be blue or violet instead of green? A long suffering sigh echoed through her head. She giggled. *"No, really. We just fade into the grasses and leaves."*

"Girl, that's enough. Boots, dresses, hair. We have to get you something else to think about."

"I could think about Deacon."

"Arrghhh. That's it. I have something else to take care of. Behave yourself."

She swam to the reeds and waited for Deacon to start down the path. *This is stupid*, she thought. *I get ready for him, and he can't even see me. I don't know why I'm doing this.* But deep inside she did. She was madly, hopelessly in love with Deacon. *It doesn't matter I've only known him for a week*, she thought. *It seems like forever.*

Her thoughts were interrupted hearing Deacon's familiar singing as he approached, and she went to meet him.

"Hi, Deacon."

"Hi, sweetie. I never thought I'd get here today. One thing after another and a small argument with this stupid girl—"

"So here you are. And look who you are with. Poor Alison, still trapped to this stupid old spring. I should have known you two would be sneaking around behind my back."

"Why are you here, Emma," Deacon asked, "and how do you know Alison? Can you see her?"

"Of course I can see her. Can't you? Ha, you can't, can you? How sad. Look at that stupid look on your face, Alison. Are you in love with him? Well, we all know how this will work out, don't we?"

"Well, hello to you, too. Deacon, this is my sister. I haven't wanted to talk about her during our conversations and bring us both down. So, Emma, you finally came back to say hello to me and Cassia."

"As if. I came because I heard in town that Deacon was spending a lot of time on walks. I just knew I'd find him here. Look at the two of you. How pathetic." Emma tossed her blonde hair back and strode up to Deacon. She pushed against his chest and shoved him back away from Alison. Over and over again she pushed, continually screaming invectives at him, driving him to the edge of the bank. He threw his arms out in an effort to stabilize himself, but it was too late. With one last push, he went off-balance and started to fall.

"I wish you would change places with your sister," he cried out as he was tossed backward into the spring.

Snap.

Alison felt the last strand break inside her. The air rippled around her and a loud *crack* rent the air, its echo sounding like thunder. *"The last penny,"* that little voice whispered. *"You're free, but please remember, you have one last task."*

Alison threw her arms in the air and laughed then hugged herself. She looked at Deacon. He sat, up to his neck in the water, a confused look on his face that was gradually replaced by one of happiness.

She laughed again in joy as he got up and waded over to her. She ran into the water and met him half way. She stared at him as he began to comprehend what had happened.

"I can see you, Alison. I can really see you. You're beautiful. Is it over?" He tentatively reached out one hand, drew it back and then, finally, reached for a strand of hair that hung over the side of her face and brushed it away from her eyes.

"It's over. I'm free to go." Alison could see her smile reflected in his face as he looked down at her.

He placed both hands on her shoulders and squeezed, as if making sure she was really there. With a whoop of pure joy, he grabbed her around her waist, lifted her high and twirled, their movements causing ripples to spiral out from where they stood. She looked down, caught in the moment of being able to touch him as well. She drew her hands over his hair and head and leaned forward as he pulled her nearer. She slid down against his body and then, they kissed for the first time.

"Worth, the wait?" the little voice whispered.

"Get out and stay out," she ordered back. She distinctly heard a chuckle in her mind, and then forgot everything as she became lost in Deacon's kiss. She reluctantly came back to the present as she heard Emma's shriek of disbelief. Pulling back, she looked at the bank where Emma and Cassia stood, face to face. She watched as Emma put both arms out and pushed Cassia back.

"No. No. No. I'm not staying here. You can't make me." Emma turned and began to jog along the grass.

Crash.

She came to a dead stop and fell backward onto the ground. With a howl, she jumped up, moved forward, and was stopped dead again at an invisible barrier. A barrier Alison was all too familiar with.

"I'm sorry, Emma, but you will have to stay here and this time the enchantment is on the person it should have been attached to all along. Don't worry, you and I will learn to get along." Cassia's tone belied her words and for a second Alison sensed the shred of doubt in her friend.

"But that's not fair," Emma said in her usual snippy tone. "He didn't throw in a penny when he made that wish."

"Actually, he was thrown in and if you check his pocket, he has exactly one penny in it." Cassia smiled and brushed a wet lock of hair from Emma's forehead. "I'm afraid you'll be here for a few years until a hundred dollars in pennies are collected and someone wishes you out. But don't worry, honey, we'll put the time to good use."

Alison watched as Emma began to jerk back from Cassia's touch and hesitate. Emma gazed at Deacon and Alison. Emma closed her eyes and then opened them and stared straight at Alison. Comprehension seemed to finally dawn in Emma's face. For the first time that Alison could remember, a tear seeped from Emma's eye and trickled down her cheek.

"I didn't understand, Alison. I'm sorry."

"It's okay, Emma. Everything is going to be all right."

They threw themselves into each other's arms and hugged. They sat on the grass, and Cassia and Deacon moved away to give them some privacy. The girls spoke for several minutes before Alison asked Emma the question that had been haunting her every day over the years.

"Do you know where Mom is? Is she still alive? Did she ever know what happened?"

"The last time I saw her was about ten years ago. She was working at the Shadow Street Grocery Store and had an apartment around there. I haven't been back since." Emma looked down and at least had the grace to look abashed, Alison thought.

"It's okay, Emma. I'll find her and bring her back to visit, okay?"

Emma started to cry and dove into Alison's open arms, sobbing as if her heart would break. Cassia and Deacon came back over and together they helped both girls to stand. Cassia kept her arm around Emma's shoulders and Alison saw again an air of calmness descend over Emma.

"As for the two of you." Cassia turned her attention to Deacon and Alison. "You may not understand the full ramifications of what just happened. Remember, the enchantment changed places. Alison, you now have eternal youth, and I can extend it to Deacon. But we can talk about this later. For now, go and just be happy. You know where we are."

The enormity of what Cassia said washed over Alison and a quick look at Deacon showed her he didn't fully comprehend what had just happened. "We'll worry about that later, Cassia. Thank you."

Deacon drew Alison into his arms. "Let's go for a while. We will be back, Cassia, I promise."

Alison nodded and kissed both Cassia and Emma before turning to wait for Deacon. He hesitated a moment and awkwardly patted Emma on the shoulder, and with what looked like relief, turned away. A quick kiss on Cassia's cheek and he was back by her side, wrapping his hand around hers.

"Deacon, you have a car right?" Alison asked. "I have a little trip we have to make before this is all over. It will mean driving to Shadow Street."

"Why in the world do you want to go over there?"

"I need to see if my mother is still alive. Also, I have it on good authority that the world's best pancakes are to be found at the diner. Do you have any idea how long it's been since I have had pancakes?"

Deacon laughed. "Then pancakes it is. Let's go."

Alison pushed back her empty plate. Not a scrap of chocolate chip pancakes remained. For a moment she seriously considered ordering another stack, but thought that two orders had been plenty. For now. "Those were definitely the best pancakes I've ever eaten, and I don't think it's because I haven't had them in such a long time."

Deacon finished chewing his last mouthful before responding. "Well, at the rate you inhaled them, I would bet you haven't eaten anything in a long time. Didn't you eat while you were there?"

"No, we didn't have to. I tried explaining chocolate to Cassia, but she had never eaten any. Can you imagine living for a millennia without ever once tasting it? I'm going to eat chocolate every day of the year."

"You'll get a fat ass, silly. Cass gave you eternal youth, not eternal being skinny."

"Oh, you're right. I may have to go ask her for an add-on." Alison giggled. "I wish the grocery store had known where Mom went. Still, it's a good lead that they have seen her walking around Shadow Street once or twice. Do you think we should try going to the PI they recommended? He sounds a bit odd."

Deacon paused in counting money for the bill and looked up at her. "After what we've been through, please define odd."

"Um…right. Let's go."

Alison looked at the sign on the private investigator's door. "No Zenocanths?" she questioned. "What in the world is a zenocanth?"

"I think it's a big bug," Deacon responded.

"Actually," a deep voice sounded over their shoulders, "that is left over from the previous owner of this place. He ran a private investigation and dating agency out of this place."

Alison turned around. In front of her was the tallest person she'd ever seen. He even towered over Deacon.

For some reason the thought of Viking ships and old stone ruins came to her mind when she looked at him.

"Um...and why would he need to specify no zenocanths? How many would just walk in from the street?"

"You'd be surprised. The last one that did was the reason he sold this business to me. I dropped the dating agency though. Do you have any idea how hard it is to work with some clients? I mean take vampires for instance. Everyone knows the half-dead can't be videotaped for the dating interview. Issues of filming aside, vampires need to lighten up and stop being so...well...dead."

Rather than think he was weird, Alison was enthralled. For some reason, she believed every word he spoke. There was something about him that made her trust him. Kind of like Cassia, she thought.

She laughed and held out her hand. "I'm Alison, and this is Deacon. I'm here to see if you can help me find my mother. I've been gone for quite some time. The Shadow Street Diner said you might be able to help us find her. Her name is Amy Raines."

"Well this is an easy case. I won't even charge you. Come on in. I'm Niklaus by the way."

"I don't understan—Mom!" Alison ran to the older woman sitting behind the reception desk.

"Alison? Alison? My darling girl, I've waited for you to come back for so long. I never gave up looking for you."

Alison and her mother laughed and cried and hugged, oblivious to the two men standing by the front door.

Alison stood at the sink in her mother's apartment. The afternoon and evening had been spent catching up with her mother and explaining everything that happened. Her mother had taken in everything and believed it.

"You wouldn't believe some of the things I've seen with Niklaus' business," she had said. "This is tame compared to some of the things we've had. Just last week we had a case that involved issues at the outdoor market. It seems there is a hellhound that lives around here with a penchant for chocolate and sweets. Oh, the trouble that one was."

Alison had looked at her mother. "The hellhound's name wasn't Smokie, was it?"

"As a matter of fact—"

They had both giggled over that one. Alison rinsed another glass and put it in the strainer, then grew still. Her mother was in the dining room clearing off the table and humming a tune. A tune Alison knew all too well. Suddenly she knew what her last task was.

"What's that song you're singing, Mother? Where did you hear it?"

"Niklaus sings it all the time. He said it was something his lost love used to sing to him. I feel so sorry for him. He truly mourns her."

"Mother! Deacon! Hurry before it gets dark. We need to get Niklaus."

Without a question, her mother grabbed her purse and Deacon his car keys. They raced to Niklaus' tall Victorian house at the outskirts of Shadow Street.

Alison raced along the path, pulling Niklaus by the hand. She ignored his protests and only urged him to move faster. "Hurry, hurry. I promise you, you need to see this."

"All right. All right. I'm hurrying. What is it—Cassia, Cassia is that you?"

Alison stood and watched as Cassia stopped brushing her hair in mid-stroke and went still. She turned and when she saw who stood before her, the brush went to the ground as Cassia went into Niklaus' embrace.

Snap.

With that sound, Alison knew her last task was completed. She smiled when she heard the voice in her head once again.

"Thank you, little one, for honoring my last request."

"You seem to know and be able to do anything. Why didn't you bring Niklaus and Cassia together sooner? They have had so much pain and sorrow. She thought he was dead and he thought she was as well."

"I'm an observer, a muse, a helper. If I went and changed everything to be perfect, what good is living? We all have to learn and grow and sometimes part of a life is to teach others. I try to right a few wrongs here and there when I am able. This is one of those times. Go and be happy."

"Goodbye."

"Oh, I didn't say goodbye, now did I?" the inner voice chuckled. *"We'll meet again."*

Alison giggled and looked up. Cassia and Niklaus still held each other tightly. Alison knew the oceanid's curse was lifted and now she could be with her one true love. Emma stood to the side, hugging her mother. Both looked happy.

And as for her. Deacon stood on the bank waiting patiently. He smiled and held out his hand. She ran over to him and, together, they walked up the path with the sweet smell of wildflowers on the breeze.

One thousand pennies to go…

"Oooh, a wishing spring," the girl's voice said. "Do you have a penny?"

"Sure, honey. Here you go," a male voice responded. "Make a good wish."

Kerplunk.

"Nine hundred and ninety-nine more to go," a little voice whispered in Emma's head.

"Who are you?" she asked.

"Let's just say you and I are going to be good friends. I have a lot of things to teach you, but first I have to tell you about this couple I know and their hellhound, Smokie. Have you ever seen what happens when you feed peanut butter to a hellhound?"

She smiled, content to sit back and listen to the story, and wait.

Timeless

Eternally Be Mine, Valentinus

Bob Nailor

Timeless

Eternally Be Mine, Valentinus

First, let me introduce myself. My name is Julia Claudine. I know it is an unusual name but my history is unusual.

I was born on the third day of October in the year of our Lord, 246. Yes, you read that correctly and so you may completely understand, read my tale closely.

My father was a simple man and served as a jailor in the courts of the great emperor, Claudius II. I was born blind and the first seventeen years of my life were a living hell. Being blind, I was forced to sit outside the front door of our small house and beg coins from those who passed by. My hearing was acute but nonetheless I couldn't tell who or what came, only that somebody or something approached. I learned to hug the wall and keep my feet well tucked up under me. Still, I never knew when a Roman soldier would rush by on a horse or in a chariot and slap my hand, causing me drop what few coins I may have collected.

It was an exceptionally hot day when my father came home and I heard him tell of the priest they'd moved from one of the jails and placed under his command. Christians, especially the priests, were persecuted and many of them executed. This one had been living in the catacomb jails for nearly two years and was one of the youngest, barely twenty.

"It is said this priest can perform miracles," my father whispered. "He supposedly married a couple and when he blessed them, the male who had a limp, no longer had it."

"Why do you tell us this, Evander?" My mother's voice was sharp. "We're not Christians."

I listened to the plates being placed on the table along with the spoons and cups. I could smell the fresh bread my mother placed to the left of me. Shortly afterward, I could hear the creak of the handle on the large pot and I could smell onion and other ingredients.

"Claudia, do you not find it amazing these Christians have miracles?"

"It is the last of the chicken," Claudia said, ignoring her husband's words.

"It smells good, Mama," I replied, and reached out to pull a section of bread away.

My father grabbed my hand. "What is this?" He softly ran his finger across the red welt.

"It is nothing, Papa," I replied. "I was begging coins when my hand was slapped with a stick."

"Nothing?" he bellowed. "My daughter is blind and gets assaulted? Did you see this happen to her, Claudia?"

"I was at the market," she replied.

I listened as my mother ladled the stew into the bowls.

"I can't take Julia with me and fight with the marketers at the same time. So she stayed home to beg as a blind and good daughter should."

My father gently caressed my hand. "My poor, poor, darling daughter."

I pulled my hand back and placed a careful finger over the rim of the bowl to test its contents. The heat registered quickly and I didn't burn my finger.

"Perhaps you should take Julia with you," Claudia suggested. "She could sit at a table and string beads which I could then take to the market to sell."

"Do you wish me to lose my head, woman?"

I wanted to giggle at my father's words, but kept silent.

"If someone were to come down into the bowels of the Earth to visit and see her sitting there…"

"Place her in a dark corner, husband. She has no use for light. Who would see her then?"

"I need no candle, Papa," I said in hopes he would consider the idea. "A flask of water and a meal when it is time to eat is all I need. I can string beads in the dark and none will see me."

"Perhaps it is a wise idea," Evander said. "Allow me to ponder its value during sleep. Tomorrow I may take Julia with me."

As I stepped out of the house I realized it must be very early or an overcast day for I didn't feel the sun on my face.

"Papa? Is it to rain today?"

"Hush, my daughter," he whispered. "We must make haste and arrive at the jail before any may see you."

I held onto my father's shoulder as he walked quickly through the streets of the city.

"Steps," he said softly.

The coolness of the walls and a dank scent assaulted me and I knew we must be getting close to the jail as he had described it for me to see within my mind.

"Here," my father whispered. "Sit on this stool and use this small ledge to hold your supplies." He lifted my hand to allow me to feel the ledge and I placed my flask of water there. "Keep silent and do not leave this stool, Julia, for your life depends upon it. There are two prisoners nearby in cells. One is a priest named Valentinus, the other is a blood sucker named Shaddius. I will return with your midday meal."

I smiled but knew my father couldn't see it if I were indeed in the darkness of a corner. "Thank you, Papa." His footsteps retreated into the distance. I pulled a thread from my bag and began to string beads. The silence was uncanny. I could hear a distant drip of water and the rustlings of things moving which I suspected to be the prisoners.

It was on my fifth string when I heard footsteps approaching. I'd been softly humming when I realized there was an extraneous sound. It was the scuffling sound as if one was being pulled along while another led. I quit my humming, leaned against the moist wall, froze and held still, not moving a muscle. My mind raced at a possible discovery of my location.

"Awake, Shaddius, you foul creature of the night," a voice growled. "I have brought you a treat. This one ridiculed the emperor so he dies at your hand per the emperor's command." A key clanked loudly followed by the hinge creak of an opening door. More shuffling. The deep voiced person laughed and I heard the metal door clang shut. I listened to footsteps fade into the distance from which they'd first come.

Timeless

I sat there, straining to hear. There was a struggle and muffled grunts, groans and sounds when an unearthly scream ended abruptly in a gurgle. It was followed by a hasty slurping sound. My heart pounded. I opened my mouth to scream, but my tightened throat was silent. I kept my seat.

"Jailer's daughter," a soft voice called from the left. "Beware the evil so near you. My name is Valentinus and I am a priest in the service of our Lord."

"Be silent." The voice came from my right. It was smooth and lyrical. "You offer eternal life after she dies. I can offer eternal life now."

I listened to the maniacal laughter of the second voice and a shiver coursed down my spine.

"Is not your name Julia?" Valentinus asked. "Your voice is pretty. Speak to me."

I frantically played my hand on the ledge in search of the flask, and grabbing it, I took a drink of cool water before wiping the back of my hand across my lips. I nervously placed the flask back on the stone outcropping. I paused, waited and finally began once more to thread beads in the silence. I finished my fifth string of beads.

"Julia?"

There was a transient heat and I realized my father had come and carried a torch.

"I have brought you food," Evander said, and placed it on my lap. He carefully touched the flask and I could tell it still held water. "I will be back later to take you home, my daughter. You are doing well with your strings. Your mother will be proud."

I heard him move toward the left to the priest's cell. "Valentinus, I offer you only the crumbs I have left," Evander said. I heard him toss something into the cell. "Eat."

"Jailer," Valentinus called. "Do you feel just in leaving your daughter in darkness?"

"She lives in darkness, Priest. Your so-called god plagued her at birth with blindness."

"I can give her sight," Shaddius whispered with a smooth voice from the darkness. "Bring her to me and she will see again and be perfect."

"Stay in your chair until I come," Evander warned. "Do not wander in this darkness, my daughter." He held my hands in his. "I will be back."

"Jailer, leave the torch so I may bask in your daughter's beauty."

"My eyes see better than yours," Shaddius said, and snickered. "I can behold her beauty without the light."

"Even though my daughter is free, all three of you are in a prison of one kind or another." Evander turned and headed away. "I will return later, Julia."

I felt the heat dissipate. Even though I tried not to smile, never before had I been told I was beautiful and now there were two who wanted to look at me. I grabbed another thread and started to string beads. My heart pounded at the excitement and I began to hum.

"Your voice is like an angel's harp," Valentinus said. "Each note lifts my heart up in great expectation only to float to the earth like goose down."

"A pity she has no idea what you say, Valentinus," Shaddius said. "Blind from birth, she has never seen what you describe."

"Come, my child," Valentinus wooed. "Allow me to touch you and give you sight so you may enjoy the beauty of life."

I remained on my chair and continued to string beads. To my right I could hear Shaddius thrash about in his cell before going silent.

"Julia, I only wish to gaze upon you," Valentinus pleaded. "Come closer."

His voice was tempting, but I had to obey my papa and I remained on my chair.

As I started on my twelfth string I again heard the sounds of somebody approaching my location. I stopped, held my breath and waited.

"My daughter," Evander said. "It is time for us to go home. Come."

"Until we meet again, my dearest Julia," Valentinus called. "I await your radiant smile."

"Whatever is that madman talking about?" Evander asked.

"He claims I am beautiful and he can make me see," I said with a giggle.

Again, the next morning I followed silently and quickly in my father's footsteps and was once again in the dungeon's jail of darkness.

"Kind jailer," Valentius called. "Please leave a small torch for me to gaze upon your daughter's beauty."

I heard my father grunt then pause in his steps.

"It is a meager light, good jailer, but it allows me a view. I thank you."

I sat on my chair in my darkness and began to thread the beads onto the strings. My mother had chastised me the night before because she had hoped I would be able to do twenty strings per day.

Today I applied myself and quickly moved the beads on to the string.

"If you could see, it would be easier," Shaddius cooed.

"Come, my Julia," Valentinus called. "Let me touch your eyelids and give you sight."

I remained silent and gave my full attention to the beads. I needed to please my mother and if she wanted twenty strings, then I would try to give her twenty. I began to hum to block out their voices.

"Your angelic voice lifts my heart," Valentinus whispered. "Your heavenly face radiates so brightly even the torch's light wanes in comparison."

I shook my head at his silliness. The beads clicked as they wiggled their path down the strings to strike one another. I continued to add new ones. Soon the clicking sound was almost instantaneous and I knew the string would be finished. It was then I noticed the silence except for scurried sounds of Valentinus in his cell.

"I shall write you a short ode," he suddenly announced.

"One she will never read, Priest," Shaddius sneered. "Even if you give her eyesight, she doesn't know how to read."

I heard Valentinus search his cell, and then the sound of rending fabric came to my ears. I wanted to imagine he was ripping his garment but I knew it was more likely from another source, one I didn't want to surface in my mind. I was curious as to what he would use to write with.

"Ah, you tease my thirst," Shaddius said. "Such sweet, untainted blood you have, Valentinus."

In the darkness with my beads clicking to punctuate the silence, I smiled as I visualized Valentinus within my mind. I'd felt the faces of my father and mother and with them to guide me, I slowly built the image of the man who claimed to love me. He would have the strong and firm facial structure of my father yet have several softened features like those of my mother. Suddenly I had an urge to reach out and touch the man, to see with my hands what my eyes could not behold.

"Your voice lures me," I said to Valentinus. "Your promise of sight is tempting." Then I turned to the creature of the dark. "Your voice terrifies me, Shaddius, yet it beckons to me in a way which I am not familiar."

"Come to me, dear Julia," Shaddius said. "I offer more than eyesight."

"Here," Valentinus called. "It is an ode of undying love written especially for you, penned with a piece of straw dipped into my very life force. Your beauty has struck a cord within my heart." He waved the small piece of cloth in the dark, damp air. It flapped making a soft sound.

I set aside my beads and stood. With hands outstretched before me, I groped in the darkness for the item he waved. I wanted whatever it was he claimed he'd written for me. His hand touched mine and I locked my fingers around the small scrap of fabric.

In the darkness of my blindness I stumbled back to my chair. The piece of fabric clutched tightly in my hand, I suddenly felt bars and again hands grabbed me. A breath of stench overwhelmed me and I knew it wasn't Valentinus who held me.

"And now, my dearest Julia, I offer you my blessing," Shaddius whispered. "A kiss." The two words were barely audible.

"Don't befoul such beauty," Valentinus screamed.

I felt myself yanked to the cold bars of the jail and then there was a heated breath on my neck. A quick prick of my skin, and Shaddius gently suckled, his tongue flicking to lick my seeping blood. A feeling of rapturous bliss overcame me, my stomach churned and it was followed by a shudder running a course of shivers down my spine.

Suddenly I was released and a euphoric fervor danced through my body.

"Two more kisses, dear Julia, and you will be able to fully see your love," Shaddius hissed.

I heard him move to the back of his cell.

"What goes on here?" Evander yelled, as he approached. "Why are you standing?" He set the torch in the wall hanger and quickly helped me to the chair. "I have brought you a meal."

"Bring your daughter to me, Jailer. I can give her eyesight," Valentinus offered.

"Silence!" Evander bellowed and glared at the priest in the dim torchlight.

"Your daughter has been—"

"You know not what you speak," Shaddius roared at the bars of the jail. "You claim to be able to give her eyesight."

For the first time in my life I could see shadows and movement. I watched as my father grabbed the torch and swung it in an arc at the two opposite jail doors.

"I said silence." My father roared at the opposing cells then helped me to the stool. "You, my daughter, will remain on this stool until my return. Never get off this stool. Am I understood?"

"Yes, Papa," I whispered, and bowed my head.

"Eat your meal and I will return later for you."

I listened to my father stomp out of the catacombs.

"Yes, Papa," Shaddius mocked. "Dear Julia, I can give you so much more."

I glared over at Shaddius' cell and could see shifting shadows, movement and outlines I'd never seen before.

"Your face gives away the secret," Shaddius said. "Already you can see some of what you've never seen before."

Valentinus scrambled to the cell door and stretched an arm in her direction. "In the name of the Lord, please, dear Julia, allow me to touch your eyes and give you sight."

"I will remain silent and diligently thread beads for my mother to sell," I said. "All I ask is for you to be quiet also."

"Would you like me to recite the ode I wrote?" Valentinus asked.

"Do as you wish," I replied, hoping deep inside he would since I'd never be able to read what he'd written.

"To see the beauty of your face

As you move to me in love's grace

To give my love, a heart afire

To live beyond my funeral pyre

Eternally be mine

Valentinus"

I slowly reached down and grabbed the cloth he had given me and brought it to my lips and nose. I inhaled, smelling the musk of him and the image I had conjectured filled my mind.

"He plays with your heart, Julia," Shaddius whispered, this time more in my head than in my ears.

"Be silent." I lowered my head, stuffed the cloth under my cord belt and began to once more string beads. It was then I remembered I was to have twenty strings ready by day's end and already over half the day was gone.

I hummed to create a rhythm to string the beads and hasten the process. My fingers were nimble and soon I was working on the nineteenth string when I heard someone approach from the distance.

"It is time to go home, my daughter." Evander's voice echoed in the tunneled chamber.

I saw a filtering of light and realized it must be the torch. My hand went out instinctively to touch it.

"How many strands have you completed?"

"This is number nineteen, Papa," I said, and faintly saw the outline of my father for the first time. A tear welled up and I felt it tumble down my cheek.

"Jailer," Valentinus called. "Let me touch your daughter's eyes and she will see."

"Why would you do that?" Evander asked. "I am not a Christian."

"To save her. Let me give her sight."

"If you think you can heal her, try."

I felt my father grab my arm and lead me over to where I'd heard Valentinus' voice.

"You are crying, my love," the priest said. "Let me touch."

In my shadowy vision I saw a figure before me.

I felt wet fingers press on my eyes and I jerked away.

"The Lord works in mysterious ways and made a blind man to see," Valentinus murmured. "My love, be not afraid for I give you the miracle of sight."

I could see the outline of a man but I couldn't see any better. "Take me home, Papa."

The next day I sat in the darkness listening to the two men stir about in their cells. I worked on the strands of beads for my mother and didn't even bother to hum. My eyesight wasn't any better and I waited.

"Can you see?" Valentinus asked, his voice soft and pure.

"You mock me," I barked, and snapped a bead onto the string. "I am still the little blind girl." I strung another bead. "Tell me how beautiful I am." Another bead. "Tell me how you adore me." Another bead. "Write me poetry." Another bead.

"I can give you sight," Shaddius whispered. "You know I can because you can already see things."

"Shadows," I replied, and nervously grabbed a handful of beads.

I was mad at Valentinus, yet I was drawn to his voice and the image in my head now had more detail. I had seen him outlined in the light. Shaddius scared me and when he spoke, a shiver coursed up and down my spine until I could clear my head of his words.

"Julia, my love," the priest called. "Come to me and let me put my fingers upon your eyelids and give you sight."

I reached up to grab more beads when the pouch flipped over and I could hear them spilling out on to the stone floor. They rolled in all directions and I needed to find them so I could continue the strands for my mother.

Cautiously, I got down on my knees and played my opened hand on the floor to search for the beads. When my fingers touched, they would roll, but I'd snag them as quickly as possible. I moved about the darkness in search of the escaped treasures.

A hand grabbed me and I was overcome with nausea for I already knew I'd strayed too far in the direction of Shaddius' cell.

"This, my dear, is the second kiss," he whispered and pulled me close.

The lips were gentler, but the experience was revolting as I felt him bite my neck. I listened to him suckle at my throat, swooning, weak, and overcome by the sheer magnitude of Shaddius. The cold, stone floor felt comforting.

"Shaddius, you spawn of Hell," Valentinus screamed. "What have you done?"

"She lives, Priest. I have no desire to kill."

"What goes on here?" Evander yelled.

"Your daughter dropped some beads and was attempting to collect them," Shaddius said. "I offered those which came into my cell and she seems to have fainted. I don't believe she realized I was that close."

"Get back!" Evander bellowed. He shoved the torch in the direction of Shaddius.

"Julia, my love," Valentinus beckoned.

I smiled at his words. This total stranger was swooning at my beauty that until yesterday I truly did not believe. I stood with my father's assistance and I listened as he hastily collected the stray beads from the floor.

"Be more careful, my daughter," Evander whispered in my ear. "My dearest Julia, is it wrong to bring such a young child like you into the catacombs?"

I reached out for the stool and in the flickering light could make out its shadowy outline. It was then I realized a truth. I could see clearer than I could earlier. Indeed, Shaddius' kisses gave me eyesight. He was telling the truth. Or was it Valentinus' magic which now made it possible for me to see shadows?

In my mind's eye Valentinus stood tall, his short cropped, curly hair was the perfect foil to the heavy brows and deep set eyes. I even remembered seeing him with a beard. The man who spewed poetry to me glistened in my mind and in the distance, beyond the flickering light of my father's torch, I could see the same figure hunched over in the distant cell. I smiled.

"You smile, my daughter?"

"At Valentinus' words," I replied.

"Be wary, child," Evander said. "You are young and unlearned in the ways of the world. Be not tricked. Sit quietly and string your beads."

"I shall, Papa." I placed my hand into the bag and grabbed a few beads to place on the string. In the distance I could see the flickering of light as my father paused to light a wall torch before wandering back up and out of the catacombs.

"Valentinus," I called. "If it be true you love me so, I command you to create another poem for me."

"As you wish, my love," he replied, and scurried to the recesses of his cell.

59

"Look at me, Julia," Shaddius rasped. "I give you sight yet you waste your time with the weakling in yonder cell."

I glanced over to the space where Shaddius stood, making out his visage holding onto the bars of his jail. I could faintly see the two red glowing points of his eyes.

"One last kiss, my dear," the vampire whispered. "One more kiss and you will have complete vision and be able to see better than even your father." A strange chortling sound came to my ears as I realized it to be Shaddius's attempted laughter. "You will be able to see the truth."

Valentinus scrambled across the cell floor and slammed himself against the metal bars of confinement. "Be silent, you abomination. I was commanded to create a poem for my love. I have done so.

"In Spring among the pastel flowers
Your beauty holds me in its powers
Like petals of the softest velvet
I offer my love with no regret
Eternally be mine
Valentinus"

"Again, Priest, you speak of things she knows not." Shaddius paced along the row of bars watching both the priest and me.

"I know what spring flowers are," I chastised. "And I have felt velvet."

"But, child, do you know what pastel is? What color is pastel? I can show you pastel. I can show you red, blue, green. I can show you truth." Again there was that ghastly sound of him attempting laughter. "You still live in darkness. There is no color."

I sat there thinking. The beast to my right promised me truth, color, sight. The man on the left promised me undying love.

Today I sit here and stare into the distance beyond the window at the pale shades of pinks, yellows and greens of Spring and know the words Valentinus spoke to me. I wear dark velvets to protect my delicate skin from the sun's rays. The decision was a difficult one and one I should have reasoned longer.

The third kiss. Shaddius enjoyed himself and I finally had to unclench his filthy fingers from my shoulders to escape his grasp. Even today I shiver at the thought of him lapping the blood from my neck. He gave me sight.

As I lurched away from Shaddius I fell to the stone floor. Valentinus cried out to me in sheer terror of my possible death. I crawled to my knees and in the darkness could see my love, my Valentinus. He crouched in his cell, against the bars toward me. The man's sickly gray pallor surprised me. Behind me, still laughing at the situation, was Shaddius with his shining skin of silver white. Shaddius' red eyes continued to watch me.

I turned carefully to Valentinus and moved closer to him.

"My love, my Julia," he called, and stretched out his pallid arm.

There was barely any muscle tissue in his build for having spent the last two years in dark, dank prisons. His twenty year old frame was nearly skeletal and when he lifted his face to me, his drawn eye sockets were dark shadows in the leprous facial skin.

I faltered. I froze in my actions and stared at the repulsive sight before me.

The man I'd envisioned, the man I'd seen in my mind was gone. Here was a creature—a frail, hideous thing with rotting flesh—calling my name, spouting words of love and poetry to me. I was appalled and a shiver coursed through my very being, chilling my soul. Shaddius had given me sight. Shaddius had given me truth.

My eyes blurred, my vision failed. I was again blind and I could no longer see.

In the distance I could hear Shaddius snicker in the far corner of his cell. "You have had the sight. You have seen the truth. You have your love. You will live forever."

Shaddius was right. I have lived forever. At Valentinus' death, his undying love returned my eyesight. Years have passed and the memory of the man I'd seen within my mind softened to include the reality of the man who loved me. I have this small scrap of cloth and have loved but only once in my long life and he had signed it...

Eternally be mine, Valentinus.

The Gate of Ethos

E.M. Shelton

The Gate of Ethos

Almost complete. The last piece of the puzzle would be in place before the dawn of the new day. Fitting. He would be a new man. Carter held the soft delicate stone in one huge fist. Bits of dust and ash rained down, startling him out of his fantasies. He relaxed his grip and set the crumbling relic on the crude altar, amidst a sea of ancient odds and ends he had collected over the last twenty years. The culmination of his life's work. He squinted in the dim light of the dying fire. He would have to add more peat before he began the ritual, but for now he was content to revel in the near silence and allow his imagination to wander. Fiona had been more trouble than she was worth, really, but her screams had subsided to low sobs that were easy enough to ignore. He felt at peace for the first time in his life.

He gazed at his pitiful supply of peat. The fuel had become scarce since the government had imposed a ban on imported goods from the Orient in an effort to stop the Black Death from entering France. Flanders had followed their lead and the massive peat mines in Antwerp had lain dormant since. Carter was lucky to have this small heap. He wasn't concerned, though. The fuel would be more than enough.

With a contented sigh he rose to his feet and began to arrange a pile of visually unremarkable stones in a circle on the altar. They looked like the kind you might find in your garden or on the hillside during a walk, but Carter knew better. He had spent twenty years tracking the stones. There were thirteen of them, none of them fitting into the igneous-sedimentary-metamorphic trifecta. Each stone was heavier than other stones of similar size, and a gentle heat radiated from their cores. Many ancient texts mentioned the stones in passing, but it took a skilled scholar and naturalist to sift through the accounts, pinpoint the stones' precise locations, and extract them without incurring their wrath. They, too, had to be summoned from beyond. As with the other relics littering the altar, the stones had a mind of their own and had proven to many to be quite dangerous.

Once the stones were arranged to his satisfaction Carter began the summoning. It was a well-cherished myth that demons could only be summoned during an eclipse, or planetary alignment, or specific time of night. The denizens of Hell cared not for the turnings of the cosmos or the position of the sun in the sky. Their realm wasn't located in the core of the Earth, as his persecutors believed. They existed apart, separated by The Gate of Ethos, the portal between the ethereal plane and the realm of mortals. Carter placed a small disc of gleaming black metal on the altar, muttering a few words into the growing dark. The disc brightened for a moment before sinking into the rough-hewn table. Carter smiled, reaching out with one hand to toss more peat onto the dying embers. His eyes never left the stone ring.

A soft moan came from behind him, rising in pitch and volume until it had become a wail. Carter smiled again, but didn't spare Fiona a glance, even when her wail progressed to a series of screams. Another demon-summoning myth was the necessity of blood from a pure maiden. Blood was required, this much was true, but demons didn't concern themselves over the source of their sacrifices. Any blood would do. Carter had chosen Fiona for personal reasons.

Cristobal d'Antonges was responsible for his daughter's death as much as Carter. When Carter was a boy, the Grand Inquisitor had tried his parents for heresy. Carter had been imprisoned while his parents were tortured. The couple claimed they had been possessed, and the finger was eventually pointed at Carter as the orchestrator. Carter, anticipating the turn of events, had broken off a rusty bit of metal from his cell and managed to dig his way out through the packed dirt floor. He felt no remorse later, when he learned of his parents' deaths. But d'Antonges had made him run—through the streets of France where he had almost starved—to the heart of the woods where he had so far escaped the leering jaws of the plague, finding solace away from the rest of the world. He had studied, learned what he could from books and diaries, and had stumbled upon the legends of the demon Hecare. He had spent the remainder of his days tracking down the elusive relics needed to summon the beast. All that had remained was a victim, a heart to sacrifice. D'Antonges would have been too easy, his suffering ended too quickly. Carter had chosen Cristobal's daughter Fiona, instead.

Three fat drops of an inky black substance slid off the thin glass rod he held over the altar, plopping with a series of hisses onto the stone. Filmy tendrils of emerald smoke rose from where the drops had disappeared to join the disc in the realm beyond. At first the smoke was barely noticeable, but before long great billows of it hung in the air. He heard Fiona cough violently behind him.

"It's all right, my dear," he said soothingly. "The fumes are not poisonous. I wouldn't risk your pretty little neck before I've put you to use."

Fiona drew in breath, probably to resume her screams, but the thick smoke brought about another coughing fit. Carter preferred the coughing to the screaming.

He finished the rest of the preparations quickly. Timing was very important. When everything was in place he turned to Fiona. The chemicals in the smoke had worked their magic. She was alert and lucid, but the fight had left her body. She gazed at him, almost expectantly. Carter severed her bonds and led her to the altar. She came willingly. He raised a dagger and, with a single deft stroke, sliced her wrist. A torrent of blood fell within the stone circle, stray droplets splashing on the stones, causing them to glow. The smoke cleared and the twisted black Gate of Ethos appeared before him, sucking the light from the clearing. With another swoop of the blade Carter cut through the rib cage, exposing Fiona's still-beating heart. He held the organ up in triumph before placing it reverently on the altar. It sank into the stone. The Gate of Ethos opened. Twelve demons, twisted and clawed, flew from the portal and surrounded Carter, each dropping to one gnarled knee, heads bowed before the gate. The thirteenth demon emerged. Hecare.

He was even larger than Carter had anticipated, with great horns sprouting from his head and bending to frame his face. His coal-colored body was heavy with ropy muscle, his feet bare, with exposed claws that would have terrified a lesser mortal. But Carter wasn't afraid. He had summoned the beast. He was Hecare's master now.

"Who dares summon me from the abyss?" The lesser demons rose to their feet, fixing Carter with bloodshot stares, fangs bared.

"You may call me Master," Carter replied boldly, "for I have summoned you to do my bidding. Kneel before me!"

A rasping, grating noise filled the clearing, and it was a moment before Carter realized the demon was laughing. The lesser demons joined him.

"Fool, human! You cannot control the demons of Ethos. I bow before no one!"

This was not what he expected. The ancient texts were explicit. He who summoned the beast shall control it. "You are mine to command," he cried.

Hecare sniffed the air. "Impertinent mortal. Your sages know nothing. To summon a demon is to enter into its service."

"But the legends—" Carter stammered. "Eternal life—it was promised. Strength beyond measure—"

Hecare grinned, his teeth dripping venom. Smoke rose from the ground where the droplets fell. "You shall have all that and more, my minion." Carter's chest began to burn, then exploded in agony as a stone, identical to the ones he had placed at the altar, was ripped from his chest by an unseen force. Hecare plucked the stone from the air. With one massive claw he lifted Carter and hurled him through the Gate of Ethos. Carter braced himself for the shock of the ethereal realm, but it never came. He simply passed through the gate, landing in a heap on the other side. He raised his head with difficulty just in time to see Hecare's clawed foot disappearing through the gate. The twisted black metal swung closed behind him, wavering for a split second before disappearing from sight.

"You will be called when your service is required." The demon's deep voice pierced the blackness. Then silence. The darkness receded, and in the pale glow of the dying fire, Carter could just make out the sinuous black muscle of his forearm. He cried out, waving his hands frantically in front of his face, as if he could ward off the change. His fingers ended in claws.

Carter woke with a start from the same dream that plagued him every night. A vision of the towering monstrosity of his master danced in his head as he rose. Charred pits dotted the mattress around the pillow, much like cigarette burns. His fangs had been dripping venom again. He stood in front of the small mirror and willed his demonic shape away. He had learned long ago to revert to his human form, but still couldn't manage to control his shape while he slept. For a wild moment he wondered what month it was, what year. Slowly, his memory caught up to him, as it always did when he awoke, disoriented. The year was 2012. He had been Hecare's puppet for over six centuries now, although puppet might be a strong word. Truth be told, he enjoyed the wanton destruction that was often ordered of him. The immortality, the strength, the fear in the eyes of the humans he destroyed. In all his years he had never found a reason to care for another. There was no good to be found on Earth, no soul worth saving. So why should he weep now for the demise of the damned?

He thought back to that long-ago night. His first act, upon recovering his wits, had been to gather the body of the lovely Fiona, and dump the remains unceremoniously on the parlor rug of Cristobal d'Antonges. The old torturer had been mad with grief, and Carter had relished his agony. After giving the Grand Inquisitor a taste of his own medicine, Carter had left him in Paris to suffer through the Black Death.

The only gripe he had with his demonic existence was the rampant boredom he was plagued with whenever Hecare had no need of him. Like the past month. It was uncommon for the demon to leave him dormant for so long. Carter sighed. After a final appraisal of his human form he dressed quickly, hoping to find some excitement in the city.

Perhaps it was the French influence in the city that had drawn Carter to New Orleans when he had arrived in the United States in the late 18th century. The city was rife with the damned and he had enjoyed many a demonic hunt through its streets. All in all he was fairly content there, as close to happy as he had ever gotten. His killing sprees had not gone unnoticed in the city, either. The locals were terrified of the night and the demon that stalked those who strayed from the safety of the bright lights and crowds. Since it had been so long since his last summoning, Carter decided to seek out some sinners and take matters into his own hands. Hecare encouraged these excursions. Perhaps he would hear of Carter's enthusiasm and issue him a real hunt.

He headed down a darkened street, his eyes adjusting to the gloom immediately. Ahead of him were faint waves in the night air, like heat rising from the blacktop on a summer day. Humans. He sniffed the air. A male and a female. He slowed his pace and began stalking their movements. They had no idea he was there. He followed them down several poorly lit avenues, relishing the chase. He could hear the faint lilt of the woman's laughter and the low murmur of the man's response. Then Carter detected another sound. Stealthy footfalls following his path down the tree-lined road. Someone was trailing him. He smiled.

"Show yourself," he whispered. His voice was quiet, but it carried down the street, hauntingly clear.

A rustle of wind through the trees, the fading sounds of the couple as they turned a corner. The footfalls had ceased. Carter waited. From the shadow of an oak a man emerged.

"To what do I owe this pleasure?" Carter asked, as if the man had visited him at home.

"Demon," the man replied. "I know what you are. I've watched you hunt. Pestilence and death follows you."

Carter nodded agreeably. "This is true." It wasn't the first time a human had identified him for what he was. "And you are here to protect the swine of humanity? To fight for the good of man and all that nonsense? I suppose you are here to kill me?"

"I will send you back to Hell!" The man raised a pistol into the air. He was armed to the teeth, belts of bullets strung across his hips like a western outlaw. Carter could even make out a few speed loaders for the revolver. His smile widened. One of the perks of being immortal was imperviousness to projectiles, but he had become rather fond of the sensation of being shot, stabbed, and burned. He braced for the impact as the mysterious man, full of righteousness, fired off a single shot.

Odd.

Then it hit him. The smile slid from his lips and everything else was lost in the agony. The world faded to black.

Carter awoke, the nightmare dancing in his head. What year was it? His chest ached when he tried to breathe and sharp pain pulsed through him when he tried to move. Wait, breathe? He woke in his demon form. Why did he need to breathe? He strained to look at his body, gasping at the pain in his neck. A ragged hole pierced his decidedly human chest, a mixture of red blood and black venom surrounding the puncture. What on Earth had happened?

Footsteps. Different from the man with the gun. Softer. He willed his body into its demonic form. The pain intensified, his skin turning momentarily black and distorted before fading back to human. He heard a soft gasp from beside him. With every ounce of strength he could muster he turned in the direction it came from. A young woman stood beside him, eyes wide. She recovered quickly and took a seat on a small wooden stool.

"Hold still," she told him. "You'll only hurt yourself."

Without another word, she plunged a long, thin metal object into the hole in his chest, pulling it out a moment later with a look of triumph. The flattened remains of a bullet, like polished obsidian, clinked against the tray she deposited it in.

"You're lucky to be alive," she said.

"Who are you?" Carter rasped. "And where am I?"

"You are in my flat. My name is Evelyn. And, if you don't mind, I have some questions of my own. What are you?"

The question didn't surprise him. He was dripping venom, for one, and he was sure she had seen his feeble attempt at transformation. What surprised him was how calm she was, as if she nursed wounded demons every day. He noted, for the first time, she was wearing gloves. He hoped he had burned her meddling fingers.

"You've been phasing in and out," she went on when he didn't answer. "If I were to wager a guess I would call you Demon, though I suppose the term would have different meaning to different people."

"Why aren't you afraid of me?" Carter managed to get out.

Evelyn sighed. "You hardly seem in any condition to harm anyone. Perhaps I should have left you to die. After all, what's to stop you from coming after me, should you recover? But I couldn't just leave you there."

"What happened?" Carter asked. His breathing was no longer coming in gasps and he struggled to sit up. The pain had subsided quite a bit with the removal of the bullet. Evelyn took advantage of his semi-upright positioning, wrapping several thick strips of what appeared to have once been a sheet around his chest. A few stray wisps of smoke rose from the bandage where the venom touched it before smoldering. Evelyn watched curiously.

"I'm not sure. I was driving by when I saw you in the street. There was a man leaning over you. At first I thought he was helping you, but when I got out of the car he was shouting some crazy story about killing a demon." She smiled weakly. "I suppose he may not have been crazy, after all."

"How did I get here?" His vision was clouding again and he quickly reverted to a supine position.

"I had a bit of trouble getting you into the car," she admitted. "You're awfully heavy. When I got here I put you in the wheelbarrow. You've been asleep for hours. I'd have removed the bullet immediately, but you were—" She couldn't seem to find the words she wanted, so she gestured at the scorch marks on his bandage, instead. "I couldn't get near it until the— bleeding stopped."

"Why did you help me? You knew I was dangerous. An idiot could have figured that out."

Evelyn shrugged. "We can't help what we are," she said softly. "Who am I to determine whether you should be left to die?"

Carter couldn't believe what she was saying. How could she doubt whether a demon should be allowed to live? Stupid girl. He started to sit up, but the pain flared again.

"What are you doing?" Evelyn asked.

"Leaving."

"Nonsense. You can't even sit up. Stay here until you get your strength back."

Carter ignored her and redoubled his efforts. This time he made it to his feet before the world went gray and he fell to the bed.

"So you think this was the culprit?" Carter asked for the twentieth time. It wasn't that he doubted her theory. Quite the contrary. He, himself, had seen the glistening black metal, had once held the relics. He had seen the Gate of Ethos. But why was the black metal of the ethereal plane here, in New Orleans? And how had that mystery man known to use it?

"I think if I hadn't gotten it out of the wound you wouldn't be here right now. I wonder where he got it." Evelyn regarded the small slug with curiosity.

She was right. If she hadn't removed the slug, Carter would be dead. Or whatever passed for dead to a demon of Ethos. He surely didn't want to find out.

Carter shifted his attention from the anomaly in his hand to the one sitting across from him. She wasn't beautiful. Not by Hollywood standards, anyway. Her hair was a mousy brown, long and straight. She was an octoroon, with smooth skin the color of almonds and clear blue eyes. A light spray of freckles dotted her nose, making her seem younger than she was. For the past month she had tended to his broken body, had been his constant companion. He had resisted mightily the first few days, but eventually he had to admit, to himself at least, he needed help. He was in too much pain.

As the days progressed he had found himself more and more grateful for her company. She was a scholar, specializing in medieval history, and knew quite a bit about old legends. And she was fascinated to hear firsthand accounts of Europe during the Black Death. She asked him openly about his origins, how he had become what he was, and what it was like to be immortal. More interesting, still, was his willingness to answer her inquiries. She didn't fear him and wasn't repulsed by him. By the end of the first week he had begun to look forward to their conversations and he would plan things to discuss at night before he dropped off to sleep.

Today they were speculating about the bullet that had sapped his strength and nearly killed him. It was definitely of the substance Carter had dubbed Ethos steel. It would have taken a special production line to manufacture ammunition based on the metal. More troubling was the fact about the obvious difficulty of obtaining materials from the ethereal plane.

Unfortunately there was another issue bothering him at the moment, distracting him from the enigma. His chest was healed. Though still slightly weak, he could move around with ease and had even phased in and out of demonic form several times, much to Evelyn's delight. It would be time for him to go. He was amazed at how things could change in such a short time. Before he had met Evelyn, the best night he could imagine involved terrorizing the locals and cutting down the dregs of mankind. Now he wanted nothing more than to continue their conversation. Evelyn had filled a hole in his empty world he hadn't known existed.

"You could stay," she said suddenly.

"What?" He must have been quiet for some time. Evelyn watched his internal struggle with a faint look of amusement.

"I said you could stay. There's nothing in the rules saying a demon from the abyss of Ethos must live alone and have no social life, is there?"

Carter smiled. "There is not."

He thought about his life and what it would mean to involve her in his work. He thought of Hecare and his gristly assignments. Evelyn didn't cringe when she touched his hard black flesh and she didn't look away when he phased, but how would she feel once she had seen him kill? The smile slipped away. He didn't think he could bear to see her look at him with fear and shame.

He reached out to touch her face, tracing a gentle arc over her jaw line, his hand coming to rest at her chin. "I can't stay. But I will come to see you every day for as long as you will allow me."

Evelyn nodded, as if she had anticipated his answer. She got to her feet, standing on tip-toe to plant a soft kiss on his cheek. "You do as you must. And I'll be here if you need me."

Carter awoke from a new nightmare. Evelyn had been in Ethos, the lesser demons tormenting her while Hecare grinned in the background, his hulking frame towering over the tiny human. He woke with his fists clenched and bleeding, dripping venom onto the hardwood floor with a pop and a sizzle. He shook the dream from his head and stood.

When he began to sway, his first thought was he might still be weak from his long injury, but when his vision blurred and the familiar pounding voice filled his head he knew better. Hecare was calling. He waited for the Gate of Ethos to materialize, then silently slipped into the ether.

He was greeted by the twelve lesser demons, much to his surprise. In the last six and a half centuries he had only seen the demons together when they were summoned by some poor, unsuspecting human. Usually the human was killed, but on rare occasions Hecare would introduce the mortal into his service. Carter had been the last human to be granted immortality in over a millennium.

Contrary to what he had been led to believe his entire mortal life, Ethos was a beautiful place. The streets were like volcanic glass, smooth but not slippery. It was a dark place—demons needed little light to see—full of spiraling buildings, massive underground cities and spectacular light displays when the ethereal realms were agitated by outside forces. There was no hot or cold and the sky was filled with dark billowy clouds of deep cobalt, charcoal gray, and indigo. The clouds bathed the landscape in their colors.

Carter approached the citadel, kneeling near the entrance. The lesser demons followed.

"Come forth," the grating voice of Hecare boomed. The glossy metal-bound doors opened.

Inside was a room which had always reminded Carter of King Arthur's round table, with a demonic twist. Fourteen chairs surrounded the table, the one at the far end, farthest from the door, huge and ornate like a throne. Carter took his place, curious as to why all the demons of the realm had been summoned. Hecare sat last. Immediately he glared at Carter.

"You have been injured," he stated. "Explain."

The lesser demons looked about as nervous as any creature with five-inch fangs possibly could. Carter stared back at Hecare calmly while he recounted his confrontation with the demon hunter, his disbelief at the damage the bullet had caused, and his unprecedented month-long recovery. He didn't mention Evelyn.

"In the past," Hecare announced, "the beings of Ethos have overlooked the passing down of demon lore by humans. The practice has been encouraged, even. The misinformation has led to countless summoning and provided Ethos with much slave labor and servitude. It is not often demons are required to destroy folklore, and even less often does a mortal represent a danger to our existence."

A soft murmur ran through the assembly, quieted by a fierce glare from Hecare. Carter listened intently. When the lesser demons were silent, Hecare continued.

"There is a demon hunter who has discovered one of the properties of what Carter calls Ethos steel." Hecare held up a small chunk of black metal. "The steel is used to bind us to the ether, to separate our realm from the mortal Earth. An unfortunate side effect of this property, if the metal becomes lodged in our skin, it begins to rip us apart. Carter has had firsthand experience with the phenomenon. It is—not pleasant.

"This human, this demon hunter, has a manufacturing plant in the United States where ammunition is being produced using Ethos steel. We must destroy this factory, and the man, and anyone who is aware of the fatal properties of Ethos steel."

The lesser demons nodded their agreement. All around him fangs were bared and claws were extended. Those with wings fluttered them in nervous excitement. All seemed ready to answer the call to arms.

Carter remained still. It didn't take long for Hecare to notice.

"That does not conclude the discussion," Carter said quietly.

Hecare nodded for him to go on.

"You overlook another issue, perhaps of even greater importance." He glared at the lesser demons. Stupid, foul creatures. He hated them all. But there was one he vowed to destroy. Who was it?

"Where do you suppose a human would get his hands on massive quantities of Ethos steel? It is not a substance of Earth, nor is it found on Earth in great quantities. The only trace of it is in the relics left for the summoning. Hardly enough to supply a munitions factory." Carter's voice lowered to a growl. "So which one of you spineless snakes transported it? Which of you seeks to undo us all?"

Carter looked to Hecare. The demon's eyes had gone milky before they slipped closed and he sat as if in a trance. The lesser demons cowered in their chairs. Strange symbols appeared in Hecare's skin, raised black on black. Thirteen stones flew from nowhere and circled his head.

Hecare's eyes flew open. "You."

Two stones fell into his outstretched palm, the rest disappearing to wherever they had come from. With a grinding of metal on metal, two of the assembled chairs clamped around the wrists and midsections of the lesser demons occupying them. Hecare held the stones in the air, ready to crush them in with one massive hand.

"Wait," Carter said. He had the feeling he knew what would happen if Hecare destroyed the stones. And he was sure it was exactly what the defectors wanted. Hecare looked at him expectantly. After an initial period of standoffishness, Hecare and Carter had come to respect each other. Enough so to instill a bit of jealousy in the other lesser demons. Carter was the only one Hecare would allow to interrupt him.

"Death is what they want. For them and for all of us. Therefore, death is too good for the traitorous bastards." Hecare grinned an awful grin. Carter had never seen a demon grow pale before and would have denied it was possible, but he witnessed for himself their inky black skin growing ashen. Whatever Hecare had in store for them, he was sure they deserved every second of it.

Carter visited Evelyn briefly before heading to New Mexico where the munitions factory was located. He had kept his promise to her, visiting every day, even if for just a moment. There were times when he thought he might love her, but he would quickly push the thought away, for what kind of future might they have together? He refused to drag her into his world.

When he left her, unfolding his jet black wings and catching a smooth zephyr toward the west, another alarming thought occurred to him. Evelyn was going to grow old. She would age while he stayed trapped at thirty-five. She would die. No, he couldn't allow himself to love her. Nonetheless, his train of thought had put a damper on his mood.

By the time he entered the munitions factory he was in the foulest disposition he could remember. He was glad to have an enemy to pursue, a direction to focus his frustration. His senses were on overdrive and he heard the quiet click of the crossbow as soon as the bolt was released.

He turned toward the sound, snatching the black-tipped bolt from the air. He hurled it at the power control switch on the far wall, hoping for the best. His hopes were answered when the Ethos steel reacted with the metal wiring producing a small, but powerful explosion. The lights went out.

A hum and a whirl and the backup generator kicked on. The crimson glow of the emergency lights filled the factory, distorting the shadows and confusing the eyes. But Carter could see perfectly in any light. It was a small matter of time before the demon hunter was in his sight. Carter smiled. The man had donned a pair of infrared goggles. If he had upgraded the device to night vision he would have had a much better chance. Carter forced his body temperature to recede. Another perk of immortality—your circulatory system was what you made of it.

He crept closer, the poor human shamefully oblivious of his approach.

When Carter stood less than two feet away he raised his temperature back to normal. He heard the click of the crossbow immediately. Despite having every intention of killing the man, Carter was impressed. No gasp, no scream. No hesitation. A shame, really. This man was a cold killer. He would have made a great demon. Carter's arm snapped out, his claw closing around the pitiful weapon until he heard the metal snap and the wood splinter. He slowly raised the hunter by the neck. He could see his enemy's face clearly in the red gloom. It was Carter who gasped.

The man was the very image of Cristobal d'Antonges.

Carter could hardly imagine such dedication. The hunter was clearly d'Antonges' heir. Had the family hunted him through generations and centuries?

"You may kill me, but my mission will live on. The d'Antonges family will purge the demons of the Earth!"

Carter shrugged. "Have it as you wish." He hurled the hunter in the air, like a baseball, catching him by the ankle as he fell and propelling him across the factory. d'Antonges crashed into the wall with a sickening *thud* and a crunch of breaking bones. Carter saw the rack of crossbow bolts seconds before the body hit. He doubted whether the Ethos steel on the tips would affect the hunter the same way it had Carter, but he also doubted the man could survive being impaled by over fifty bolts. Carter sighed. He hated to see good talent go to waste. He wondered whether the young d'Antonges knew what an evil man his forebear was.

His mission completed, Carter signaled to Hecare. The familiar dimming occurred around him, made stranger by the pale red glow. He stepped through the gate into the ether.

Hecare awaited him, grinning his demon grin. He glanced behind at the other lesser demons, their number dwindled to ten. "Destroy the factory," he ordered. "And every text mentioning the Ethos steel."

The demons departed in a whirlwind of black and gray. Hecare turned to Carter. "You've done well, though I doubt you were presented with much challenge. I have another task for you."

His clawed fist held out a scroll. Carter took it and awaited instructions.

"This is a list of all who know of the metal. Find them, hunt them. Kill them."

Carter nodded. He was anxious to get back to the Earth realm, to Evelyn. He had much to tell her. Hecare dismissed him with the wave of a giant hand.

It wasn't until Carter stood on Evelyn's porch that he realized the implications of his task. Evelyn had looked after his injury. She had removed the bullet, herself. All those conversations during which they had speculated. He snatched the scroll from his belt, nearly ripping it in his haste. The list was short, six names in all. And there, at number two, was Evelyn. Carter sank to his knees. It couldn't be!

She knew something was wrong. He hadn't been very adept at hiding it. He was distant, torn between the need to see her, to ensure she was safe and the need to stay away, to concoct some plan to thwart the inevitable.

She entered the room, bearing a tray of tea, and took a seat across from him at the tiny table. Her hand slipped into his.

"You can tell me, Carter. I won't think any less of you."

But he couldn't. How could he tell the woman who had saved his life that her reward was to be death? He had thought briefly of appealing to Hecare, of assuring his master that Evelyn was no threat. But he knew what the outcome would be. Hecare would not risk his brood. In the end there was only one thing he could do. And he would have to be ready soon. Hecare would be contacting him tomorrow to see how his mission fared. It was his only chance.

"Evelyn, I have to go away for a while."

Evelyn nodded. She didn't ask the details of his job, but she knew what it usually entailed. "That's nothing to be upset over. When will you return?"

Carter blew out a shaky sigh. "That's the thing, my love. I'm not sure if I will return."

He watched a battle rage behind her eyes. In the end she whispered, "Must it be done?"

"Yes," he replied adamantly. He only hoped Hecare's other lackeys were as useless as he had always thought them.

Ethos. Knowing he might never see its beauty again gave the place a whole new meaning. He would have to play this carefully. Hecare could pluck Carter's intentions from his mind, if he had any reason to doubt him. One slip would seal his fate and, more importantly, Evelyn's.

Hecare met him at the citadel gate. He looked positively irate. Wonderful.

"Six targets I assign you," he bellowed. "Six! An entire day wasted and not a single target destroyed. What in the Abyss of Ethos have you been doing for the whole bloody day?"

Carter dropped to a knee in subordination. "Master," he replied. "I have not ignored your request. A text has surfaced which required my full attention."

"What is more important than my demands?"

"The text is a scholarly journal. It elucidates the properties of a certain metal. My lord, the text was about to be published worldwide."

Some of the tension left Hecare. "It has been destroyed?"

"Yes, Master. But it mentioned another cache of the mineral on Earth. I have tried to discover the location, to no avail. I have come seeking permission to use the locator."

Hecare nodded. "I think that is wise. You did the right thing, prioritizing the mineral. I'll feel better once the entire realm of Earth is purged of that cursed metal."

He led the way through the citadel. Carter followed, trying his best to hide his smile.

"The locator cannot leave the city," the demon said. "You must find the cache before you leave here."

"I understand."

Hecare led him to a small antechamber filled with gadgets and gizmos of all sizes. He handed over the device, a small square slab rather reminiscent of the CPU in Carter's computer, without argument. Carter had been afraid the larger demon might insist on locating the mineral cache for him. Trust, apparently, went a long way. If not for Evelyn's imminent demise Carter might have felt a little twinge of guilt at deceiving his old comrade. Instead he gripped the locator tightly between two large fingers, closed his eyes, and focused his will into the machine. But it wasn't the made-up cache of Ethos steel he sought. No, what he was looking for was much smaller. A totally unremarkable, rather unique stone.

When the locator finally spit out the answer to his query he was not surprised. He opened his eyes and nodded once at Hecare.

"You know the location."

"Yes, I do."

"Then find it, my minion. Destroy every remnant of the metal on Earth. But beware those on the list, who know of its power." Hecare turned to exit the narrow antechamber. Carter sucked in a deep breath and drew the dagger from its hidden sheath. Hecare froze. He knew. He knew what Carter meant to do. But it was too late. The smooth black blade pierced through the demon's back. Carter covered his eyes with one wing as venom sprayed from the wound, searing his face and filling the small chamber with smoke. He snapped the hilt of the dagger sideways until he heard the brittle blade break.

Hecare raised his arms to retaliate. His eyes had gone milky once more, and Carter was afraid. Hecare's body lunged as the blade's metal poison ripped through him. Carter grabbed hold of an arm and, ignoring the searing venom, flung the beast to the ground. He had no idea how long the metal would take to kill the demon. He had lodged into Hecare's spine about twenty times the amount of black steel that composed the slug that had pierced him. The smoke increased until Carter couldn't see and the smell was hideous. He gathered the acrid air into his lungs, choking a little on the smoke, and blew his demon's breath across the room. The smoke was ejected into the hall and Carter could see the stiff demonic form, dead on the floor, milky eyes wide open. Odd. Carter had lost the ability to maintain his demon form when the metal had taken hold. He wondered vaguely if Hecare was the only demon in Ethos who had never been human.

Carter leaned over the body of his adversary, and the closest thing he had ever had to a friend. He held a gnarled hand over Hecare and whispered, "I have vanquished you. You are master no more."

A dull glow issued from the body, growing stronger and brighter until fourteen stones hovered above it. They gravitated toward Carter's hand, each one sinking into the flesh as soon as it touched. The last stone strayed from the course, floating for a moment in front of his heart before it, too, sank into the skin.

Carter turned away. He could feel the lesser demons. They were his, now, to control. He tried to pinpoint their locations. They came easily.

"No!" he cried. Without knowing how he did it, he summoned the Gate of Ethos to take him to Evelyn. Apparently Hecare had been more suspicious than he had thought and had taken matters into his own hands. Carter prayed he wasn't too late.

Carter had only a moment to contemplate Evelyn's crumpled body lying against the wall before the demons were upon him.

"Stop!" he bellowed. The lesser demons froze.

"No," gasped one. "It cannot be."

Though the demons remained frozen they had erupted in whispered conversation. "He would have to defeat the master…Hecare can't be dead…he will kill us for sure…" Carter ignored them. He knelt before Evelyn, lifting her battered body from the floor. She seemed to weigh nothing at all.

"No," he sobbed. Without much hope he checked for a pulse. Nothing. She was gone. In the span of a month, she had become his entire reason for living. He thought of the world without her. It held no joy, no discovery, no laughter. Only the emptiness of loss. He had no idea how long he stayed like that. When he rose the lesser demons cowered before his anger, as much as a demon can cower when he has been commanded not to move. Carter knew what he would do.

Cradling Evelyn's body he lifted a hand into the air. A glow and a ripping sound produced the stone from his chest. He touched Evelyn's face, his monstrous fingers tracing every line, every curve, counting every freckle. He held out the stone to her chest. As soon as the stone began to sink into the flesh he hurled her though the Gate of Ethos.

Carter fell to the floor, weak and human. It took the lesser demons nearly half a minute to realize the stone that controlled them had passed beyond Carter's reach. They descended on him in a hoard.

"Halt!"

The demons froze once more. Carter looked up at a female demon, the first he had seen. The ropy black legs had retained much of their feminine shape. The lines of her face were still visible, but a bit harsher. A fine set of horns grew from her head and a pair of inky wings flapped behind her, larger than she was. She had fixed the lesser demons with a hateful glare.

"One shall live," was all she said.

It took the demons another long moment to figure out what she meant. When it finally dawned on them they began to rip at each other, desperate to be the one to survive. Evelyn passed them by without a second glance.

Carter smiled at her as she approached. Blood oozed from the massive gashes the demons had torn in his body. Evelyn fell to her knees beside him.

"You gave it up for me?" This time it was her hand on his face.

"I don't want to live in a world without you," Carter replied.

"But there's no need." She held up a hand, fourteen stones appeared, five of them crumbling to dust before her eyes. She shot a quick glance over her shoulder. Five of the demons had lost the battle thus far. "There are nine stones left. Surely you can absorb one of these foul souls?"

"It doesn't work that way, my love. You can only sacrifice your own stone."

Tears flowed down the demon's face, splashing to the floor in great burning drops.

"Hecare wanted me to kill you," Carter explained. "I couldn't. I love you."

The demon held him tighter. She opened her mouth to reply, but snapped it closed a moment later. Carter's body had gone limp.

The twenty-fourth century. The wonders of technology never ceased to amaze Evelyn. For all the changes that occurred on Earth, Ethos stolidly remained unchanged. She absently tossed a stone into the air. It was a rather unremarkable stone, yet there were only two of its kind. The other resided deep within her, and she'd be damned if she ever let anyone get to it.

Three hundred years. She had thought life would become bearable again if she let just a year pass. Perhaps then she could find something to look forward to, some reason to wake in the morning. When a year had come and gone she thought perhaps ten. Then twenty, one hundred, two hundred. Then she had decided. If after three hundred years she still felt the pain of Carter's death, if the emptiness had not been lessened, something would have to be done.

And here it was. The three hundred year anniversary of Carter's demise. Of her own demise as well, if she thought about it.

"Cathos!"

The air was sucked out of the room and quickly replaced as the last of the lesser demons was transported to the ethereal plane. The creature cowered before his mistress.

"Yes, madam?" He had to repeat the reply. The first had come out a barely audible squeak.

Evelyn smiled. It was the first smile to have crossed her face in three hundred years. The lesser demon shrank away from it. "It is time, Cathos."

Cathos' skin paled to ash, but all he managed was a meek, "Yes, mistress." He disappeared through the gate.

Evelyn sat at a small table in one of the citadel's antechambers. It was the same table that had once graced her flat in New Orleans. She rarely crossed the plane to Earth anymore. She set the silver tea service on the table and poured two cups. She gazed at the empty seat across from her.

"You always said you hated the world until you met me. That the Earth was only bearable if we could share it. You were right, my love." She raised her cup in a salute to her long-dead companion. "To the end of the world," she toasted. "May it bring peace to us both."

She sipped her tea, waiting for Cathos to return. The steamy liquid did not warm her. When she felt the lesser demon's stone stir within her she opened the Gate of Ethos. The demon offered her a small white box.

"You have leave to enjoy your last moments however you see fit," she instructed the demon.

Evelyn turned back to the empty seat. "You wouldn't believe the technology they have on Earth now, Carter." She waved the little box toward the chair. "We thought, once, that the hydrogen bomb was the worst thing mankind could have come up with. But you must see *this* little gem in action. It's never been tested, of course. How could it?

"This, my dear, is the detonator for the new photon fusion bomb. Rather brilliant, actually. A small explosion upon detonation, and it actually absorbs photons. Light. The blast should be enough to destroy the entire Earth and, theoretically, the rest of the cosmos. So out of curiosity, I've decided to see if such a device will affect Ethos."

Evelyn sighed. "It'd all be over then. I guess I didn't want to live in a world without you, either."

She pressed the smooth black button in the center of the detonator. A blinding white light encompassed her.

The Boy and the Nymph

Matthew Borgard

The Boy and the Nymph

As is often the case, there was once a boy. This particular boy lived long ago, in the days when fae, goblins, and unspeakable creatures of the night had yet to be driven from the world. But this story is not about such horrible things.

The boy was a stout lad, possessed of strength and size even before his eleventh year. He was the son of the village woodsman (an ox of a man himself) and had recently taken up learning the family trade. The boy accompanied his father's team on many expeditions. They slew trees and animals alike, bringing bounties of each back to their people and winning praise on their return.

But the boy was not content to watch. He wanted to help the men with their work. And so, as was the custom, he was sent into the shadows of the deep forest with nothing but an axe, a spear and a chain, and told to bring back as much wood and food as he could manage. This, of course, was a trick. A boy could chop down the biggest tree he could find, but he would not be able to drag it back to the village. He could slay the largest, most succulent boar in the forest, but even the strongest of men would not be able to carry it alone. The best of the woodsmen understood that a pair of doves in the village were better than the largest elk rotting in the forest.

The boy was as arrogant as he was unripe, and he did not understand the test. He stomped into the forest, looking for the highest and tallest trees. Each time he found one, he would stare up to the heights, shake his head, and move forward. "I've seen Father cut down trees twice as big," he would say to himself. The men told legends of towering pines that pierced the clouds, and the boy wouldn't stop until he found one.

As the day grew darker and colder, the boy's legs began to tremble. His hunger made him weak, and he knew he wouldn't be able to go farther without stopping to hunt. He scanned the ground, searching the soft mud for tracks. It didn't take long for him to spot a hare cowering in the brush nearby. The boy reached for his spear, but the hare was too smart for him and ran off before the boy had his weapon in hand. He gave chase, for even with his tired legs, he knew he could outrun a rabbit. It took him around a hill, over a damp patch of grass and through a cluster of trees. A stump appeared in his path, catching his foot before he could change his direction. He threw out his arms as he fell, but it did not stop his head from striking the rock nearby.

The boy awoke in a grove surrounded by a cool mist and the sound of trickling water. His head ached, and as he started to sit up, a warm, gentle hand pushed on his chest.

"Not yet, man-child. You should move slowly."

She was a small thing, but not frail. A green hue flowed through her skin, from her fingers to her toes and everything in between. Her dazzling, sun-painted hair trailed behind her like a serpent, and a necklace of gems and bones hung from her neck. She wore a shaggy dress the color of autumn leaves, cut just above her knees. The boy couldn't look away. The girls in the village did not dress that way.

"What happened?" asked the boy.

"I found you in my forest," she replied. "You took quite a fall."

The boy snorted. "This isn't your forest. It belongs to our village."

The nymph was not angry at the boy. He simply did not understand. "Would you like to eat?"

"I would. But the rabbit got away."

The nymph giggled. At her touch, the tree closest to her lowered one of its limbs, and from the tip of the branch sprung a plump red apple. The boy preferred meat, but he was starving, so he took it without a word. When he was finished, the nymph could see that he hungered still, so she summoned another fruit, and then another, and then another, until the boy was filled to bursting. He leaned back, then, and his eyes fell on the most glorious sight: an oak, twice as wide as all the rest, and taller than any he'd ever seen. This was what the woodsmen spoke of.

"My axe," he said. "Where is my axe?"

"Your things are there. But you won't need them. I can give you anything you want. You need only ask."

The only thing the boy wanted was the tree. He took his axe and stepped toward it, but that was not something the nymph would allow. "You cannot have that one. That is my tree; that is where I live."

The boy was thick and burly, and the nymph was small and feminine. If he wanted the tree, he should have been able to take it by force. But her tone made it clear that such transgressions would not be permitted. "Please," he said, "I need to prove my skill to my father."

The nymph did not enjoy dealing with the people who entered her forest, and she was glad that they kept far away from her home. But she heard honesty and innocence in the boy's voice, and so she did not shy away from him.

"You may not have this tree, but if you leave it as you found it, I will offer my help to you. What do you require to pass your test?"

The boy considered the question, and then responded. "I must bring back the tallest tree and the fattest boar. Then they will make me a woodsman like my father."

The nymph tittered, her voice like the feet of thousands of insects rampaging over fallen twigs. "And how would you carry this tree of mine, man-child? You are strong, but you are not that strong."

The boy did not like this. Even if the nymph was right, he could not allow anyone to doubt his strength. "I could roll it. Even if it took me all week."

"You are a silly child. Let me give you what you need."

"That will not do. It is cheating."

The nymph flitted closer, leaning her head on the boy's shoulder. "The other men told you to take the wood and the meat from the forest, yes? I am the forest, man-child. I will give you the wood and the meat."

The boy was stubborn, but the nymph's words rang true. If the forest offered him what he came for, how could he turn it down?

"I am grateful for your help," the boy told her. "But which tree shall I take?"

"You will go to the watering hole, away from the morning sun's home. There you will find what you seek."

The boy was satisfied. Dreams of being the town hero flashed in his head. "Thank you, spirit. How can I repay you?"

The nymph danced around the boy. She had never been asked such a question before. There were not many things she wanted that she did not have. But tending to the boy had been entertaining, and she imagined she would enjoy the chance to speak with him again. "Return here," she said at last. "Return here on every cycle of the moon. I am lonely. The beasts and plants bow to my touch, but they cannot offer me companionship. My sisters have all fled. I am the only one left."

The boy agreed. He had hoped, even before the nymph's deal, that he would be allowed to return.

The nymph pushed her face close to his. "But you cannot tell the others about me, man-child. For if they find me, they will seek to cut down this tree, and then I will die."

"I promise," said the boy.

The boy walked toward the setting sun, as the nymph had instructed. There, at the water hole, he found a herd of aurochs drinking happily. Cords of ivy attached the beasts together, and three massive logs, already topped and delimbed, spanned their backs. The boy, having no interest in husbandry, wondered how he would guide them back to town, but to his surprise, they heeded his every command like well-trained dogs. It took only a few hours to return to the village, and with his veins filled with the invigorating fruit from the nymph's trees, the boy did not even stop to sleep. The villagers were astounded, and they begged him to know how he accomplished such a task. The spirits were kind, he told them.

Though the boy was as skilled a woodsman as any his age could be, the villagers demanded he replicate his feat. And so, as the moon returned to its full splendor in the sky, the boy returned to the nymph as he promised. The nymph exulted, for she had not expected to see him again.

The boy had thought only to ask for more gifts and return to the village, but seeing the nymph's home with a clear head, he found himself entranced by the beauty. The verdant shades of green and shining blue hues were deeper here than near the village, the trees taller and the odors more potent. He had been dazed the first time he awoke here, unable to appreciate the splendor, but now he stood in awe.

"You are incredible," he told her. "Did you create all of this?"

"Some of it, but not all. The deep woods existed long before I was born. I am but its caretaker."

The boy and the nymph spoke for hours. He told her of his family, and of his work as a woodsman. The nymph had seen him, of course, as she saw everything that happened in her forest. But she did not tell him this, as she did not want to appear too bold. Instead, she told him just a handful of her many secrets. She told him that a blooming moon-lily meant rain the next day, and that disturbing a dead sparrow portended tragedy. She told him that many of the animals in the woods were just like the men-creatures. They nested, mated for life, and died. To her, the boy was just another one of the forest's residents.

When the sun had set and the birds had retreated into their nests, the boy mustered his courage and placed a kiss on the nymph's lips. He had never kissed any of the village girls—it was not allowed before marriage—but his passion and the

The Boy and the Nymph

nymph's beauty overwhelmed him, and he could not control himself. The nymph, unfamiliar with such human customs, did not know how to respond. But the boy's embrace made her feel warm, and she did not object.

Before he left, the boy asked for another gift. The nymph gladly obliged, since the boy had made her feel happier than she had since her family left her. The boy returned to the village with a flock of wild sheep, baskets of the juiciest fruit any of them had ever tasted, and enough cut lumber to build a house. The villagers asked again for the boy to give up his secret, but he would not tell them about the nymph. He wanted more than ever to keep her to himself.

The boy's monthly visits turned into weekly, and then to daily. The nymph showed him her secret places in the forest, and the boy showed her tools and crafts from the village. He told her he would take her there, someday, to introduce her to his family—though he did not know how he would make good on such a promise. The nymph's gifts continued, allowing the boy to outshine his peers. He became the pride of the town, and the village mothers bickered amongst themselves to present their daughters to his family.

Days and months passed, and while the boy grew into a fine young man, the nymph remained ageless. When the boy reached his fifteenth year, it came time for him to choose a wife. All the girls of the village were trotted out in front of him. Some were beautiful, some were skilled, and some were not. But all the boy could think about was the nymph. As soon as he could manage to sneak away, he escaped into the woods.

"They say I must choose a wife," he told the nymph.

She was hurt by the boy's words, though she did not know why. "Of course. It is good for all things to have a mate."

"Deanna cooks well, but she is too fierce for my taste. Yua is soft and quiet, but she cries often, and for no reason at all."

The nymph listened to his words intently, even as she feigned focus on the restless lizards nearby.

"I do not want any of them," said the boy. "There is only one I wish to make my wife."

Even with the warm breeze, the nymph felt cold. "And what is her name, man-child?"

"Her name is the winter's snow, the early spring's storm, the sun's rays in the summer. Or so she has told me."

The nymph leapt into his arms, sending them both tumbling in the grass. She layered kisses upon him, as she had become quite comfortable with that particular ritual. "But what will the other men-creatures say?"

The boy had expected this question. He had himself thought about it. "They will gossip behind my back. My parents will be angry. But they cannot throw me out. Not as long as your gifts continue."

"And they will, my love. For as long as the sun rises and the rivers flow."

The boy and the nymph were wed under a canopy of petals and stars, beside the nymph's life-tree. The nymph's friends, the rodents and birds, were their audience. The boy did not invite his family. Their lives were good, for a time. The boy only left the nymph's side for logging expeditions, which were rarely necessary because of the nymph's generosity. The nymph did not mind, since she would live an eternity, and so a few days of his absence made no difference to her. The boy carved ornate animals for her, and she appreciated them as much as a creature of her kind could, for, though the boy was creative, the nymph had witnessed the creation of oceans and mountains.

The time came, however, when the boy grew restless. He witnessed the other men and their wives in the village. He smelled their home-cooked meals and became jealous. The nymph did not understand the concept of crafting a meal. She believed it was strange to modify what the Earth provided. The boy saw the women greet his peers as they came home, and he found that no loved ones awaited him. The boy watched as the new children appeared at the breasts of their mothers, and this was what hurt the most.

It had been a year and a quarter when the boy's frustrations conquered him. He came to the nymph with a heavy heart, and he could not bear to look her in the eye. "I cannot stay any longer."

"Another expedition, so soon?" asked the nymph.

The boy had prepared his speech, but it was still difficult. "You cannot give me all that I need."

The nymph fluttered around him. "What do you mean? Do you not get warmth from the fires you start with my wood? Do you not dull your hunger with the fruits I grow for you? Do you not quench your thirst from the ponds that spring up at my feet?" She felt an anger rising up inside of her. She did not like his rudeness, but if the boy wanted more from her, she would give it. She loved him.

"You give me all that and more, and I am grateful. But there are things you cannot give me. You cannot give me the comforts of a home. You cannot give me the loving embrace that a wife gives her husband, and you cannot give me a child to carry on my name."

"I can try. Please, let me try!" The nymph felt a withering in her chest. The boy was right. She could make many things, but she knew she could not create a child.

"I blame myself. We are from different worlds. I should not have asked this of you."

The tears attacked the nymph's eyes like angry honeybees. She did not understand why the boy was being difficult. None of the human girls could match her. She could find a way to make him happy. "You told me you hated all the other girls. Who will you marry?"

"Milanda, the seamstress's daughter, is newly widowed. She is without children."

"Is she as beautiful as me?"

"No," the boy admitted. "There is nothing I have seen in this world that is as beautiful as you."

"Will you visit me?" the nymph asked, the desperation growing in her voice.

"I will not. Not after I marry. It would not be proper. This must be the last time we see each other."

The finality of the boy's statement mystified the nymph. Her world was one of renewal, of a constant cycle of death and rebirth. The idea that she would never see him again was not just confusing, it was frightening. And the nymph had never been frightened. "But you cannot leave. I love you."

The boy loved her, too, but it was not enough. After he left the forest, the nymph wept. She wept for days, for weeks. The poisonous tears of misery flowing from her eyes spread through the land, feeding the flora and the fauna alike. Each became weak and shriveled, and as the months went on, the woodsmen found their bounties smaller and smaller.

Soon the nymph's tears dried, for she had no more sadness to give. But she listened to the boy when he came into her forest, and she found her sadness replaced with rage. She followed him, just out of sight, tracking his every step. Every time his axe bit into wood, he would find it hollow and rotten inside. Every time his spear would pierce the skin of an animal, he would find it sick and infested with larva. And every day he would curse his misfortune. But he did not return to her. And then, suddenly, he was gone. The nymph did not see him in the forest anymore.

Even as the seasons changed and the moon cycled back and forth in the sky, she did not forget about him. But her anger had not subsided, so when the boy finally returned to her home, she hid from him.

"Come out," he yelled, poking his head into their secret places. "I want to speak with you. Come out! I beg of you!" The boy screamed for hours, but the nymph did not come. "You think I have not seen your work? Your vengeance follows me like a stray cat. Without wood, my family freezes. Without food, they starve. You can punish me, but do not punish them. They have done nothing to deserve your malice."

The nymph did not care. She no longer had any sympathy for the men-creatures who defiled her forest. The boy called louder and longer, but still she did not appear. Finally, the boy stopped speaking. From his pack he produced the same ragged axe he had always used. With a powerful swing of his arm, he stuck the blade in the trunk of the nymph's life-tree.

It did not hurt like she thought it would. Not like the feel of a weapon in her skin. But she felt the blow in her soul, and it was not pleasant.

It is a farce. He will not do this. When the nymph did not come forth, the boy continued chopping, again and again. The life-tree's bark was strong, the boy's blade was dull, and the progress was slow. But each swing of the axe, meek as they were, gave the nymph the same ghostly shock, and at last she could take it no longer.

"You will not fell it with that pitiful tool," she said to the boy. "The life-tree grew thousands of years before you were born. Greater forces than you have failed to disturb it."

The boy lowered his axe. "You must stop this. I do not ask for your gifts or your help. Just leave me be. Let me hunt and log like any other man."

"You are not like any other man." The nymph let out a great wail and flung herself through the branches of the trees. "I once thought that you were better, more honorable. I thought you were proof that our creators did not fail when the man-creatures were made. But I was wrong. You are the worst of all of them. While they are content to take my creations and ignore me, you wanted more. You wanted to trick me, to take my gifts, to cause me pain."

"I never wished to hurt you. I was a selfish child, and I cannot take that back. But I demand you leave my family alone."

The nymph's laugh bounced from rock to rock across the ground. "You cannot demand anything from me. What if I do not do as you say? What will you do then?"

"I will cut down this tree, even if it takes me a year."

The Boy and the Nymph

"You will get no food or shelter from me. You will die before you succeed."

"I will die just as surely if I do not try."

The nymph had nearly tired of him. There was only one question she wanted answered. "Did you lie? When you told me you loved me?"

The boy looked into her eyes as the frigid wind cut into his skin. "I did not. Not once."

His answer did not surprise the nymph, but his absolute faith in his honesty did. She knew it was not wise to believe him, but she could not help it. "I will give you what you ask for. Every morning, when the first ray of sun finds its way across the mountaintops, I will leave my gift for you on the edge of the forest, where my trees meet the boundary of your village. You may take it and use it to feed and care for your family. But in return, you must promise me never to return to the woods. I never wish to see your face or hear your voice anywhere in my presence for as long as I live."

The boy was heartbroken. He had loved the nymph, and he loved her creations equally. The forest was a part of his soul. But he was a husband and a father now, and his duty was more important. "I will do as you say. You will not see me again."

And true to his word, the nymph did not. The boy no longer joined the other woodsmen in their hunts. As the years passed, he took not a single footstep into the forest. The nymph provided for him, as she promised. Every morning she would place an offering of lumber and fruits in her designated spot, and every morning it would disappear.

Their arrangement continued for years thereafter. The nymph did not forget him, but her pain dulled as her loneliness returned, and soon the nymph found herself just as she had been before she had met him. The boy was merely a single ant in an endless march. A simple mistake that could be placed behind her along with all the others.

One morning, with fresh snow blanketing the nymph's home, she felt a pair of feet marching toward her lair. She awoke to find a bearded, hunched old man trekking through the snow. She thought him aimless at first, but it soon became clear he was coming for her. She watched as he found her life-tree, though the nymph was not worried—such an old man could do her no harm. He ran a single shriveled finger along the scar from many years ago. The nymph thought it odd that the wound from the boy had not healed when so many others had. But there were many odd things in the world, so the nymph did not question it.

"I know you are still here," the old man said. "Your gifts come as sure as the rising sun each morning. Come out, so that I may look upon your face one last time."

He coughed so strenuously that it forced him to his knees. Though his posture had been broken and his muscles diminished, the nymph could see the boy for who he was. She had seen many creatures grow old and die, and it was good. It was the way of things. But this was different. It pained her to see him this way.

"Why have you come here?" the nymph asked. "You are sick and weak, and the forest is cold and treacherous. You will die here!"

A smile stretched across the boy's face. "If you could grant me such a kindness, I would die happy."

The boy collapsed, then, and the nymph was there to catch him. She cradled his head in her arms, gently brushing the chilled sweat from his forehead. She had spent a lifetime loathing him, but seeing him now, weak and fragile, reminded her of the happier times they'd shared.

"I have broken my promise," the boy muttered.

"Do not let it trouble you," the nymph replied. "I forgive you for coming here."

"But not just that. I promised I would not tell any others about you."

The nymph's eyes widened. "Whom did you tell?"

"Each day when I returned to my home with your gifts, my family would ask me where they came from. And each day, I would tell them nothing. But I could not let it die with me. I left my son a letter, telling him to find the secret here."

"Why?" asked the nymph. "I do not know your children. I do not prevent them from entering my forest. They do not need my help. They can take wood freely."

"It is not them I worry about. It is you. You have been alone so long. You should not be alone anymore."

They were the last words the boy spoke. The nymph kissed him as he passed, taking his dying breath as her own. She howled. The tears that flooded the forest were not tears of pain or wrath but tears of gratitude, for she had been given the chance to see her love one last time. His body was taken by the forest, wrapped in ivy and swallowed by the very ground itself. He would be a part of the deep woods—a part of her—for all time.

The next day, the boy's son came. He made his way to the spot his father spoke of in his letter and sat, waiting for a sign. At first, the nymph did not show herself to the new man-creature. But he did not try to cut down her tree, or taste her fruit, or bother her animals. And so, as the sun set, the nymph came out from hiding and greeted him. And then she told him her story.

The boy's son soon brought his brothers and sisters. And soon after, they brought their wives and husbands and children. It took time for the man-creatures to earn her trust, but as her fondness of them grew, so too did her compassion. She allowed them to partake of her gifts, and in return, they sang songs for her and told stories. The nymph was not lonely anymore.

Today, the nymph still lives in the forest, right next the life-tree with the shallow wound that will never heal. The boy's descendants visit her, and though she often forgets which child belongs to whom, she still knows them as family, as she can see the boy's sparkling eyes and sturdy frame in each of them.

The Trippet Stones

Kimberlie Orr

The Trippet Stones

I smell it, the brine. It brings back memories, so many memories. I am home again. I know it.

But I'll never be me, the me I used to be, no matter where I end up. The tears are starting, the way they usually do at this point. I roll over and, in doing so, get a mouthful of grit and sand. The sick, stale taste left over from earlier would have been bad enough. I try to calm myself by listening to the water. So hopeful, the ebb and flow of it...

"Alex! Are you all right? *Alex!*"

I'm fairly sure the voice is directed at me. *Alex.* Not a very helpful name. Am I male or female this go-round? I drop the slick, square bottle I've been holding and pat myself down tentatively. Hmm. A woman, for the first time since my run-in with Morgana, but not at all like I used to be. I hardly have a shape. No curves, no *anything.*

And these silly clothes. Insubstantial, sleeveless top, a flimsy waistcoat thrown over it that doesn't do anything to protect me from the raw, wet air. And jeans. Those mad blue jeans that have been everywhere for decades now. I wore them as the factory worker up north that time. Two lives ago? One? Before the dog, but after the tree. Oh, I don't know. I used to be able to keep them all straight, but now, I'm so weary at the thought of starting again. I begin to cry in earnest, hard, rough, and hate myself for doing so.

Man up, Morgana says in my ear.

"Wha'?"

Be a man.

"You should've made me one, then."

He approaches, the bloke who's been calling out for Alex—*me*—and crouches down, also in jeans and an enviously warm-looking cardigan. He's shaking his head. I reckon I am a bit of a pathetic sight. I *feel* pathetic. Smelly. Coated by strips of sand and salt.

He, on the other hand, looks pretty impressive against the heavy, pink sky. I feel my face getting hot as he takes me in. He's tall and solid…adorable, really, in a diffident, awkward way, with disheveled hair that's just getting more disheveled in this mist. And there's that medallion he's wearing—it's about the size of a 2 pence coin, with a complex pattern of interwoven knots. It's so familiar…

"*Alex*," he says.

I raise my eyes to his, uncertain. He reminds me so much of "…Thomas?"

Morgana's irritating smugness echoes in my head. *Yes. Sort of.*

"Um." I struggle onto my elbows, trying to think of something normal to say. "What are you doing here?"

He frowns slightly. "My morning walk." His voice peaks slightly on the last word. "How could you forget? You and Glen give me a hard enough time about it."

I try to concentrate, but I'm having trouble. One of the disadvantages of inhabiting someone else's body without any sort of easing in. I truly take it over, so, right now, I'm feeling the hollow, sickening swirl of alcohol in my belly. I look at the bottle I've relinquished. Ah. Jack Daniels. Brilliant. A few pale blue pills, too, damp and disintegrating in the sand. Alex was hardcore. No doubt about that.

"When I saw you lying here..." Sort-of-Thomas lets out a sigh. It's a bit shaky, more so than he probably intended. "Well, I thought that was it, you know. Our own Amy Winehouse tragedy on the Cornish shore."

He doesn't realize how right he is. You see, the inhabitation of a fully-formed entity can't happen unless the original owner is on his or, in this case, her, way out. *Rest in peace, Alex.*

"Let's get you back to the hotel," Sort-of-Thomas tells me.

There's a talent to it, by the way, of trying to find out who in the world you are without sounding too thick. It helps that Alex would've been out of it just now. I hope she would've been, anyway, after enjoying her little buffet of whisky and pills. But the added surprise of a very distracting, very attractive bloke may make my detective work especially difficult this morning. At least I know it's morning. I remember the angle of the light from so long ago—too long ago—despite the solid clouds.

He tries to help me up, but my clumsiness causes both of us to almost fall back onto the ground. I have to hang on to him...not that I mind. He feels so warm and safe. It's comforting, the soft wool of his cardigan against my cheek. Finally, we're more or less steady on our feet, and I have to make myself let go of him. "The hotel in Padstow?" I say in a careful voice.

"Padstow is tonight," he says. "And at the end of the week we play the Solstice Festival—remember? Outside Blisland." He breathes out a laugh. "Don't feel bad. Glen had to remind me, too. Sometimes I think my little brother would make a better manager than me."

"Ah. Right." So whatever it is we do consists of a lot of traveling.

The seagulls circle overhead with their arching, tangled cries. Even though they cause my head to throb, I so appreciate the sound. And the water! It has kept its teal glow, like a frosted glass ornament I remember from some point during one of my lives. Always dependable, my dear Celtic Sea. Once again, the homesickness pierces me, mixing with the residue of all that stuff in my stomach, and my eyes brim over.

Sort-of-Thomas has noticed, of course, and reaches over to me. He is guarded, though. "Are you gonna be all right?" His gaze flickers down. I'm sure he sees the incandescent blue pills embedded in the grainy ground. "Maybe we should find a doctor…"

"I'll be fine." I dab at my eyes with the top of my wrist. Afterwards, I see the runny blackness of make-up and mascara all over my skin. I cringe. I must look beyond awful. That thought makes me want to cry more, which will make my face even worse. Endless cycles. A bit like my existence.

A good man, Sort-of-Thomas. Not only does he pick up that ghastly bottle ("Recycling," he tells me apologetically), but as we scramble over and around the chocolate-brown slate jutting up from the beach, he keeps his free hand at my elbow. It hovers close enough that I can feel its aura, yet he never touches me. "I think…" He stops and is so silent, I'm wondering if I imagined him speaking at all.

"I think," he finally says again, and I jump, caught up in maneuvering my way through a particularly steep passage, "that after you have a chance to…um, clean up, we should have a meeting."

"Okay," I say.

He raises his eyebrows at this, apparently surprised by my response.

The wind, dense with moisture, whips my breath away. The hotel is in front of us now, rising from the rocky beach, with its unassuming, white stucco façade.

"Well, then." He looks at his watch and I notice that he wears no ring. So he's not married. *We're* not married. A useful bit of information, if somehow disappointing. "Maybe after breakfast. Nine or so? In the lobby?"

"Sure." Another agreeable response that seems to mystify him.

The key is in my front jeans pocket. It's attached to a hard, irritating rectangular thing that has been bothering me since I got up and followed Sort-of-Thomas away from the surf. "Number 9," I say. *Number 9, number 9, number 9.* My old master used to play that Beatles album over and over again while I lay curled up at his feet. It's one of my favorite canine memories, and I embrace it, even though Morgana destroyed everything by making me turn against him. To shake myself of this sadness, I hold the key up to Sort-of-Thomas triumphantly.

"Very good," he says, apparently at a loss. He holds the front door open. I'm so aware of him as he follows me up the narrow stairs. He is close behind, prepared, I think, to offer support if I happen to waver and fall, which is very much a possibility. And then, on the first landing, we part, me with a silly, little wave, him lifting the incongruous bottle of Jack Daniels.

My room is nice. Simple. Smells a bit like mildew, but I don't mind. I take note of a gorgeous wine-colored violin on its stand in the corner as I doff my clothes. They are worse than I realized. The sick smell grows exponentially stronger and sourer in the close, heated space. If Alex, the real Alex, had been able to expel all this poison before I took over and did the deed for her, I might be somewhere else, something else. One single action can make all the difference.

A bath. I rarely took them as the dog or the factory worker. I got rained on as a tree, but that was as good as it got. So I relish the opportunity, filling the tub with delightfully steaming water and bubble bath, which the proprietors have thoughtfully made available, letting out a long "Ahhhh" as I settle in. Of course, before I can fully enjoy any of it, Morgana, preceded by a too-sweet cloud of lavender, walks into the bathroom and appraises me. Despite the fact that she is dressed in a maid's uniform and has the gangly appearance of pale, Eastern-European summer help, it's her. I can tell by the eyes. They, like the Celtic Sea, never change through the ages. The eyes of a sorceress—slanted and icy-blue and very, very scary.

I slump forward and try to cover myself to the best of my ability, thankful for the bubbles.

"Oh, please, cousin." She holds up her hand. "Spare me the modesty."

"He looks so much…" I can't help it. My voice catches, its weakness amplified by the pre-fab walls. "Like Thomas."

"A bit more staid. Dresses like a pensioner, in fact, but yes." She takes a seat on the toilet. "He's a descendant—the great-great grandson."

So he had children and grandchildren. And found someone

to have them with. At least it wasn't Morgana. But even that doesn't make me feel any better.

"Such a delicious opportunity," Morgana says, "coming across him." She leans forward. "I have a plan, my dear. A way to make you pay for taking him away from me."

"I didn't 'take him away.' He made his own choices…" But I can't talk about it anymore. It upsets me too much. I fold into myself, the hot bathwater lapping away peacefully.

"I beg to differ," Morgana says. She puts her cold hand on top of my head. She's always touching me, yanking at me, slapping me about. "If you do this one last thing, I will release you."

I'm not sure I've heard her right. She's always controlled by threatening to hurt those I've grown close to, by threatening to hurt *me*. But there's never been an offer of freedom.

"You poor poppet! Let me wash your hair."

I give in, because, really, I have no choice. I never have a choice with her—never can refuse her anything. Her nails scrape at my skull and the suds run forward in streams, all of them, it seems, straight into my eyes. Right then, at the worst moment, she buries her hand in a swirl of shampoo and goth-black hair and jerks my head back. My eyes are on fire. I keep them shut, partly because of the stinging, but mostly because I don't want to look at her. "You make this boy, this great-great-grandson, Thomas Tremaine, fall in love with you."

"What?" I am in pain, real pain. And so confused. "He can't stand me. I can tell. He's only being nice because he has to."

"That's your problem to fix." She twists her hand in my hair. "No worries, my dear. It'll be easier than you think. As much as I hate to admit it, there's an unbreakable bond there. Neither of you can fight it."

I'm afraid to ask. "And then what?"

"And then you get that Tremaine medallion from him. But don't steal it. Make him give it to you...as a declaration of his devotion."

Back when I was myself, in my own body, in my own world, my Thomas, the cleverest, sweetest boy in Padstow, loved me. Who would have guessed? *Me*, so quiet and unassuming. He spoke about giving me a token, a Celtic knot. This made my cousin furious...and vengeful.

My voice is small. "And then what?" I manage.

"You break his pathetic heart. Run away, grasping onto his gift. Hurt him." She pours water over my head, so anything I attempt to say at this point is a blurry babble of sound. "And then..." She grasps my shoulders and turns me towards her. "I will have closure. And you will be free."

"I'll never be free," I splutter through dense sheets of hair. "I'll never see my family again, never get to tell them goodbye. I'll be stuck in this body, this horrible, drunken girl's body, in this weird century, for the rest of my life."

"It could be worse." She is holding my shoulders so tightly. I will be bruised, I know, after all this. "The girl was talented. Young—barely eighteen, I understand. There's so much potential."

I don't say anything, just stare ahead.

"And...you'll be free of me."

"Is that true?"

"Truer words were never spoken." She lets me go and

straightens the skirt of her too-big, starched uniform as though she doesn't have a care in the world. "As much as I'll miss tormenting you, I'll have to find other entertainment."

Will the freedom be worth it? I don't know if I have it in me to betray again.

"And," she adds for good measure, "your dear Thomas won't meet with any misfortune."

I should have known she'd stick to the threats as a backup. She can read me so easily, whether I have branches or paws or hands. It doesn't matter.

I wonder, as I have many times before, if I am her only victim, but I've never engaged her in a conversation about it. I talk to her when necessary, to receive my marching orders, to find out whatever meager information she chooses to tell me about my new role. But I draw the line at chatting about her hobbies.

Morgana. The daughter of a long-dead cousin. She was strange, admittedly, living on her own far outside Padstow, wandering about at the oddest times, or so the villagers said. I tried to defend her. Too naïve, me. I defended everyone, always wanting to believe the best. If I had realized how mad she was about Thomas Tremaine, I would've...well, I suppose I would've tried to avoid him. But avoiding someone in your small sphere in those days was a hard thing to do. Especially if you cared about him. And I did, as much as I tried not to.

All this thinking about the old Thomas doesn't help at all when I finally make my way downstairs to see the new one. He's in the musty sitting room, accompanied by nothing more than a cup of tea and small glass of water. His quiet presence intimidates me more than the crowd I've been expecting. My heart pounds at the sight of him, half in apprehension and half in longing, and I almost turn around and go back up.

"You're *early*," he says.

"Yes." My voice is squeaky and hoarse, barely there. I settle into an overstuffed monstrosity of a chair, the one farthest away from him, and run my fingers over the worn upholstery. It's decorated with a dizzying pattern of crowns and scepters. I spend an inordinate amount of time studying these.

"You look different," he says. We stare at each other a couple of beats too long until he shakes his head to break the spell. "Do you want to pop into the other room and grab some breakfast? There's time."

I breathe out a shaky laugh. "Ah, no. No breakfast just now, thank you."

He leans close, over the low coffee table. "How do you feel?"

I shrug. "I'll survive."

Smoothly, as though it's a routine part of his day, he slides the glass of water across the expanse of particleboard, towards me. When I frown slightly in question, he throws me the packet of Alka-Seltzer. I catch it by clapping it between my hands.

"That should help," he says, the corners of his eyes crinkling up in the most beguiling way. "Does wonders for me and Glen."

I've got to stop *looking* at him! Instead, I turn my attention to the task of tearing my gift open and plopping the tablets into the water. Bubbles erupt from the surface like fireworks on Guy Fawkes Night. The sound of it, fresh, fizzy, makes me smile. "Thank you." I raise my glass to him and down as much of the contents as I can stand, just about half, before setting it on the table again. Thomas is watching me, surprised or confused, I'm not sure. Finally, after another shake, he says, "You're welcome."

Right then, three others I reckon I should know show up. They appear to be Thomas's age, which means they're a few years older than Alex—*me*, I mean. As they settle in, a couple are staring with such strange expressions that I look around the tall back of the chair to make sure someone isn't about to drop a platter of breakfast plates on me.

"What?" I clear my throat. "Is anything the matter?"

The fair boy with the most angelic face laughs. "No war paint this morning," he says. He doesn't act like an angel at all. In fact, there's something in his expression that reminds me of Morgana. As though he's been scorned—or thinks he has, anyway.

"Oh." I touch my cheek. "I didn't know if there'd be enough time."

The red-headed one mutters, "That never stopped you before." And then a hard, resentful silence falls over the group.

Thomas pushes his cup and saucer to the side, rests his elbows on his knees and clasps his hands. "Look, we were talking last night…"

"Just tell her, Tom," the red-head interrupts, waving a pair of drumsticks at me. No doubt he'd like to slam them against my head. I take another sip from my glass, partly to appear nonchalant, but mostly because he's making my stomach hurt again. "We've had it with you, Alex. The tantrums, the drinking, the *attitude*. We're sacking you."

Bad timing on the Alka-Seltzer. When I hear this bit of news, the fizzy water goes down the wrong way.

"Drama queen," the fair boy says. "Always making a scene."

"Hang on." Through the hazy headache my coughing has aggravated, I see Thomas getting up. He crouches beside me, much as he had this morning on the beach. And then, with a quiet apology, he slaps me hard on the back. "Are you all right?"

I take a wheezing breath. "Yes. Thanks…again."

Urg. That *stare*. From all of them this time, including Thomas. They're acting as if I've grown horns or something. Sprouted wings. Shape-shifted right here in front of them.

"What's with the gratitude?" the red-head says. He's not friendly at all, despite his vibrant curls. They seem to light up the whole of this rather somber room. "Trying to make us feel sorry for you?"

I shake my head. "I wouldn't do that."

Thomas still has his hand, warm and broad against my back. "It's not that you don't have the talent. You're amazing, really."

"A bloody prodigy," the darker boy says. A skinnier version of Thomas, undoubtedly the younger brother, Glen. He's been quiet up 'til now, not even joining in the glowering.

"But," and regrettably, Thomas takes his hand away, "we're spending too much money…" He falters, trying, as always, to be diplomatic.

"…cleaning up after you," the red-head is more than

willing to offer up.

"So." Thomas grasps onto the arm of my chair, about to pull himself up. "We'll get you transportation back to London." He nods at the brusque blond. "Mike will take over on fiddle, for the rest of the tour, anyway. And I suppose I'll have to step in on guitar."

"Wait." I grasp onto his sleeve, causing him to waver and settle back into his crouch again.

"Here comes the scene," Mike says.

"No scene," I tell him. Thomas's medallion glints in the corner of my vision. I swallow. "Look. Last night was really bad. I think maybe I got too close to the edge."

Mike and the red-head roll their eyes. But Thomas and Glen are watching me. Waiting.

I should take them up on their offer. Run far, far away. But that won't save Thomas…or me. So I look at each of them, straight on, and finally at Thomas. Oh, his eyes. A lovely hazel. And those lashes. I am blushing and have to bow my head but not before I realize his cheeks have gotten a bit flushed, too.

"Give me one more chance," I say to my knees. Clad in another, thankfully clean pair of jeans. "I don't want to be the person I was anymore."

Mike scoffs, but I face him again. "I'm sorry," I say, "if I've hurt any of you."

Now *he* reddens and turns towards the foggy window.

"Please. Let me come to Padstow. You have every right to get rid of me if it doesn't work out."

"I don't know, Alex." Thomas is close, so very close. I can feel the warmth of his words. "Changing a year's worth of...behavior, overnight?"

"I can do it," I say. "Please let me try."

Two against two. Thomas and Glen willing to let me stay, Mike and the red-haired drummer, Stuart, ready to give me the boot. As I pace outside, kicking at the gravel of the car park, waiting for them to talk it out, a couple of men pass me on their way to the footpath and give me a more than polite smile. I nod, my arms folded against the mid-morning chill, puzzled. Really, there isn't much to this Alex. He had coarse, shoulder-length hair, dyed an opaque black, the rather small, unremarkable body. And without the make-up, she definitely looks like a kid. I can't fathom what these men see in her, which makes my mission of bewitching Thomas all the more daunting.

At least the Alka-Seltzer is doing its job because the watery sun isn't stabbing my eyes and causing them to throb anymore. In fact, it feels good. I lean back against the stucco, liking the roughness of it through my thin waistcoat and shirt. I must lose track of time a little. The tap on my shoulder causes me to jump.

I open my eyes and Thomas is there, staring down at me, casting me in his substantial shadow. "Padstow it is," he says.

"Really?" It's not at all premeditated. I hug him, long and tight, and after some hesitation, he wraps his arms around me, too. Maybe because it's been so long since I embraced someone, but it feels amazing and right. I have a hard time letting him go, but I make myself. "I won't let you down," I say, my hands planted against his chest, on either side of the medallion, but the sickening whirl returns to my stomach with those words.

"I'm counting on you," he says. "Get your gear, then. It's time to go."

Obediently, I run towards the entrance. Glen is leaning against the doorframe, wary, eyes intent. "He fought for you, Alex. Remember that."

I nod, not trusting myself to speak, and rush past him to gather my meager belongings.

The Trippet Stones. That's our name, and even that, like the smell of the sea this morning, brings back so many memories. My dad, long ago, always stopped by the various mottled monuments on his travels, giving me a chance to explore them if I ever accompanied him. And there was that time at the beginning of summer, when Thomas asked to tag along. While dad sold his copper pots in nearby Blisland, we snuck away to the barren moor.

I hid behind a pitted stone, breathing in the clean, moist air left over from a recent rain. "Where are you?" Thomas called out, his voice causing a thrilling little shiver to shoot through me. And then he was there next to me, spinning me round to face him and staring at me with a gravity so unlike him.

"What's the matter?" I whispered.

"You're so amazing," he said. "So beautiful.*"*

"Don't play with me." The old, reliable self-doubt surfaced, and I ducked away from him. *"What about Morgana? I think she fancies you..."*

"Morgana worries me." He frowned a bit, which only made him look more handsome. *"My mum is sure she's a witch."*

"Thomas!"

"Mum knows about these things." He pulled me close again and brushed a wisp of hair from my cheek. *"Stay confident when she's near. Hold her at bay. There's a verse to recite, something I learned as a child..."*

I shook my head. "A verse? That seems so..."

I couldn't say more because he leaned close and kissed me, the lightest brush of his mouth against mine. Without even thinking about it, I was kissing him back, all my reservations gone. He was so warm, so strong and gentle at the same time.

When we finally surfaced, and I certainly didn't want *to surface, he started to reach behind his neck. "I want you to have this." His bronze medallion glinted in the dull light. But before I could protest, before he could follow through, Morgana appeared from behind a stone, descending upon us...*

I remember feeling ill, violently so, my vision sparkling at the edges. All of a sudden, I was spinning upwards, far above the moor. I could see Thomas. He was sitting on the ground, his arms braced behind him, as though he had been pushed backwards. The expression on his face...I could hardly bear it. A mixture of stunned confusion and growing dread...

How clever of her, to find Thomas again. To bring us all back to the Stones on the Solstice for her *closure*. She certainly knows how to play her game.

On the coach, curled on a seat in the back, I look through Alex's rucksack, at first reluctantly, then with resignation. It's full of desperate stuff, at least to me. Cigarettes, loads of them; more pills, in every color imaginable. And all these clippings. The girl liked to collect articles that had anything to do with her, which is helpful if not a little sad.

Her history explained a good deal. Orphaned at twelve, but showing a startling proficiency for violin. Once she reached her majority, she auditioned for the Tremaines' Celtic band and relished being the center of attention. The rest of the year was a mess, apparently. There were run-ins with police in every conceivable part of the UK, brawls, situations, all forgiven because of her tremendous talent. Ladbroke's even started a bet that she wouldn't make it to her nineteenth birthday. *They've won,* I think. *And they'll never, ever know.*

The coach's progress is relatively smooth, even on these narrow Cornish roads, and, once I flip through pretty much all her newspaper and magazine clippings and try to sort out the gorgeous mobile phone that was carelessly bouncing at the bottom of the rucksack amongst biscuit crumbs, I find myself slipping in and out of a doze. Despite the brilliant scenery outside my window, rocky, glistening shale, the sparkling teal of the water fleeting between the trees, I can't stay awake. Yet my subconscious is too troubled to allow for an undisturbed sleep. I see Morgana, feel her hovering, waiting, and at one point, I sit up with a strangled cry. I cover my mouth, but luckily, the grinding of the tires has covered up my distress.

Well, maybe not. Thomas happens to be trundling by right about then and pauses. "You all right?" he says.

I nod, the memory of Morgana causing me to tremble.

"You're cold. I'll get you a blanket."

I start to protest, but he is gone and back before I can even form the words and throwing the flannel covering over me. "We need to get you a jacket," he reprimands and then, after a bit of consideration, sits in the roomy seat next to me.

"You take good care of us," I say.

"I try."

I think back to the articles I've just read, how some revealed that Thomas always wished he could be as talented a musician as those in the band, how he feels he does better at the arranging bookings and dealing with finances. "Have you been practicing?" I ask.

He breathes out a laugh and rests his head against the seatback. "No point."

"I can help you." I have no idea if I can do any such thing, if I can even play the beautiful instrument reverently stored away by our one roadie. But I want him to reach his potential. My Thomas was quite a musician. A singer, too. I can't seem to remember him without a pang of longing.

"I doubt *anyone* could." He looks over. "Hey. What's the matter?"

I shake my head. "Still have a headache." To change the subject, I point to his medallion. "That's pretty."

"This old thing?" He looks down at it. "They say it belonged to another Thomas Tremaine, back in the day."

My mouth goes dry. "Is that right?"

"Yes. A sad story, or so I understand."

"Tell me."

He stares past me, out the window, the shadows and

sunlight dappling his face. "He was mad about a girl. Someone he had known all his life, someone kind and sweet. He planned to give her this." He lifts the medallion, and then lets it fall back into place, silently, against his chest. "They were to be married, but one day...well, she disappeared. Just like that."

"She ran away?" And I remember Morgana's instructions to me. *Break his pathetic heart. Run away, grasping onto his gift.*

He shrugs. "No one is sure. Some claim—well, it's fantastic stuff—that she disappeared right before his eyes."

She did.

"But," I say, trying not to dwell at that moment so long ago, "he must have found someone else. Or you wouldn't be sitting here with me."

"Yes. He settled, as we would describe it today. Was never really happy again." A silence. We're both apparently picturing him, this lonely man sleepwalking through the remainder of his life. "He started writing afterwards, trying desperately to get his work published. Strange, because he never showed any interest in that sort of thing before."

"Writing?" I am mesmerized by this, wanting to know every bit of information I can.

"Yes. Mostly poems. Some are bizarre—almost like a recipe or instructions. But others...well, they're beautiful, really. Glen has posted a few on our website—he loves old, cryptic stuff like that. And we've set one of them to music. 'Return to the Stones.'" I must look confused because he nudges me. "You know it."

"Um," I say, faltering. But he saves me by reciting a few lines.

"Remember when we kissed
In the morning mist,
By the Trippet Stones?"

Of course, I don't know it...yet. But the scene set by the song, the idea of it, is so very familiar. Thomas, *my* Thomas, wrote about me—about *us*. And his words live on, even today.

"So, getting back to his sad little medallion. It's been passed down, over the generations. Mum and Glen always joke with me. I'm to give it to the chosen one, whoever she may be." The corner of his mouth lifts up and he gets lost in thought before turning towards me again. "You must be tired."

Very, I think. Years and years of weariness seem to take over, just like that.

"Rest." He reaches over and tucks the blanket under my chin. "We should be in Padstow soon."

"Okay." My eyes follow him as he gets back up to resume his watch. And then I am able to sleep peacefully.

I had no need to worry about the violin. Sometimes, a part of the entity, a residue, remains, and luckily for me, Alex left her amazing gift behind. Not only can I read the music, I can play it. But the word "play" isn't even adequate to describe my ability. During rehearsal and in The Golden Lion during our show, the ribbons of sound I create wrap around us, so rich and honey-sweet that I'm close to tears the whole time, especially during the song "Return to the Stones." It's as though the first Thomas Tremaine is trying to tell me something through that plaintive lyric, despite all the years that have passed, despite all the lives separating us.

I don't have to sing, thankfully. Mike, our front man, takes care of that. Instead, I can devote all my time to my instrument: my fingers glide and linger over the neck, my bow skims and tilts wildly in a beautiful dance. But what I find even more gratifying is that I'm a part of a unit, a tight, perfect circle of sound that includes Mike's guitar, Glen's bass, and Stuart's impeccable drumming (and those shimmering crests of sound he coaxes out of the cymbals). The audience is enthusiastic, to put it mildly. I'm a bit abashed when quite a few call out my name, and I suppose I can understand why Alex let this go to her head.

Most of all, I love seeing Thomas standing just off the stage, in charge of it all, our anchor.

Afterwards, we are welcome in the bar. Both Glen and Thomas seem worried about this, and even I am, slightly. Another residue is surfacing here at the throbbing music pumped over the speakers, the murky atmosphere—even the motion of the barman's arm as he pulls down the lever to fill a glass brings out a dizziness in me, as though I'm anticipating some sort of escape. There is just as much danger in quitting completely, I know. One of the factory worker's friends—well, he had the worst time when he stopped. Shaking, mad restlessness, a *horrible* temper. To be safe, I ask for a half-pint of lager and sip it cautiously, thankful that the taste hasn't improved over the years.

We huddle around the bar and various patrons come by and greet us. One even asks me for an autograph. I'm glad I read the articles and remember Alex's surname. As I look up, I notice that both Mike and Stuart are rolling their eyes at this exchange. They seem to do that a lot. I pull one of those very helpful articles from my back jeans pocket and unfold it. "Did you ever see this?" I ask them.

They straighten from their slouches defensively. "What?" they both grumble in unison.

"From *New Musical Express*." The words sound unwieldy in my mouth. I remember how my music-loving owner used to refer to the magazine, back when I was a scroungy mutt. "I mean *NME*. A review of our show in Penzance."

"What about it?" Stuart asks, clutching his drumsticks so tightly, his knuckles glow white in the gloom.

I point to one passage in particular. "Praise for your drumming and Mike's vocals." I make a condescending noise, a sort of *humph*, trying to maintain a little of the old Alex. "It goes into excruciating detail. Wanna see?"

Mike reaches out tentatively and when he takes the paper from me, I give him a smile, just a flicker of one, testing the waters. He doesn't smile back, but he nods. He's actually a nice-looking kid when he doesn't have that scowl on his face.

While he and Stuart read, I make myself sip the lager. Thomas and Glen are a few stools down, heatedly discussing some aspect of tonight's sound mix. I get caught up in them. In Thomas, really, how his heavy, dark hair falls over his eyes in his enthusiasm. How he pushes it back and, when listening to his brother, bounces his fist lightly against his mouth. A rather nice mouth, wide and generous.

What are you waiting for?

Morgana, in my head. Always close by. I turn towards the bar, stiff, defensive, and lean my crossed arms against it. "What do you mean?" I mumble.

Don't play innocent with me. Reckon I'll have to get the ball rolling.

Someone jostles me on the way past. I catch a cloying whiff of lavender and look over my shoulder. So does everyone else. A woman, very similar to my old self, tall, voluptuous, with long, golden hair, walks straight towards Thomas. I catch a glimpse of her profile, of those icy-blue eyes. And I know.

She taps him on the shoulder, smoldering in her silky top and leather trousers. He turns and I can see it, the admiration in his face, as he takes her in.

"Hi," he coughs out. Polite as always, he stands up clumsily, almost knocking his barstool over.

"Are you the manager of the band?"

"Uh…" He glances at an amused Glen for help, then turns his full attention to her again. "You could say that."

A coldness, as cold as her eyes, pierces me, above my stomach and right below my heart, as she presses the length of her majestic body against his. And majestic hardly does her justice. I never appreciated, before now, how lovely I was.

I'm not alone. Various patrons around me, including Stuart and Mike, murmur in approval. One even lets out a wolf whistle. "I so admire that," she says. "Keeping everything together." She pokes her long finger into his chest. "Calling all the shots in that serious, *sexy* cardigan."

"Believe me," Thomas says. "It's not rocket science."

"Shhh." Now she's resting the tips of her fingers against his mouth, the wonderful mouth I was just admiring. "I beg to differ." And then, the witch gets even closer, if that's even possible, and kisses him. Long and hard, causing the rapt bar to erupt in applause.

Hardly realizing what I'm doing, I grab hold of Thomas's sleeve and drag him away from her, past a slew of patrons, some laughing, others groaning because I've put an end to Morgana's little show. I can feel her glaring at me.

It's quiet outside, except for the faint vibrations of bass from the pub and the constant rising and falling of the sea in the distance. Relatively abandoned, too, due to the heavy rain that battered the village earlier this evening. Except, now, for Thomas and me. I feel a disorienting whirl of *déjà vu*. I used to live here, long ago. Confused and panicky, I let Thomas go, my hand just dropping away, instead of giving him the reprimanding little push I had originally intended. Not that he would've noticed either way.

"Wow." He is rubbing the back of his neck, his profile edged by light from the riotous common room. "I've never had a groupie before."

I begin to pace, crossing my arms, as I am wont to do. "Fancy her, do you?"

He steps in front of me, causing me to skid to a stop against the glistening cobblestones. "Not really. She's not my type."

"Didn't know you had one."

"I do," he says. "Now."

I'm having trouble breathing. I start to circle around him,

but he takes hold of my shoulders. They're still tender from Morgana's roughness this morning. I must have winced, because he moves away, palms up, cautious once again.

"I'm sorry." He plants his hands on his hips now and drops his head back. No lighting technician could have done any better. His silhouette framed by a corona, as though he's emitting a blue glow.

"No. It's…" I start forward, but then I'm not sure what to do next and stumble to a stop, even though I'm aching to feel the warmth of his skin against mine. "I must be sore from my little jaunt last night. On the beach."

A pause. His breath spirals out as he sighs. And then, he says quietly, "It's such a struggle for me, Alex. I don't want to be…inappropriate, but I can't…" He makes a sound between a laugh and a groan. "I can't seem to stop touching you." He takes my hands in his. "I've always wanted to protect you. But ever since this morning, there was more to it. Like I was seeing you for the first time…"

"Ugh. Bad first impressions, then. I was dirty, sick…"

"That didn't matter. Not one bit."

It's hopeless. I fall into him, and he holds me tightly, without hesitation.

"You've changed," he whispers into my hair. "Just as you promised."

Stupid tears. They seem to start up so easily, just as the rain makes its reappearance. I can actually hear the individual drops, hard and heavy, against the top of my head. I bury my face into his chest. "You've always believed in me," I said, muffled. "All along."

"Yes."

I raise my face to his and I can't help feeling disappointment when he kisses my forehead. "We should get you inside. You need a *jacket,* Alex."

I touch the medallion. It's cold and menacing and fills me with dread. And, right then, a particularly brutal blast of air whips past. Thomas tightens his hold on me. It would be better, though, if he let the wind carry me away, into the water. For the both of us.

After tonight's final show in Padstow, which couldn't have been any better, during the contented coach ride to Blisland, I turn on the mobile phone I found in Alex's rucksack. I'm not good at this Googling business, but I type in "breaking a spell." Such a general subject. And everything remotely associated with those words comes up. Personal websites of witches in the area, the lyrics of a pop song with a similar name.

Useless! I throw the mobile back in the rucksack and drop my face into my hands.

Morgana's right. Despite the fact that Thomas is sitting at the very front of the coach and I'm at the back, I can feel his concern. There is a bond there. He worries about me, and there's no doubt that I care too much about him...

If only I could find a way to save both of us. Anything. A phrase. Instructions. Where have I heard that earlier? *Almost like a recipe or instructions.* I rummage in the rucksack again to retrieve the poor, abused mobile and clumsily type in the name of our website.

It is very early on Solstice morning, the sky a low-hanging purple, threatening the festival planned for this afternoon. I pull my rucksack over my shoulders, take one last look at the room I barely spent a few hours in, and make my way out.

The little town of Blisland is quiet. I catch a glimpse of myself in a shop window, hardly knowing who I am any more. Not the old me, certainly, with this slight frame. But not really Alex, either. After a couple of thorough washings, the black dye is starting to fade. What a pain it must have been for her to maintain. My hair, as it turns out, is not at all dramatic. It's brown, just brown, with a bit of a wave, if that.

I walk and walk. I remember the way from before. The narrow roads. The heavy trees becoming sparser as I approach the moor. It's all familiar, yet different. My heart starts to pound, a little sickeningly, as I scramble over a rise.

There they are. The stones. Scarred with lichen, worn by weather. But still impressive, despite everything.

The wind is tearing at me. I walk up to a stone, lean my forehead against it, welcoming the roughness against my skin. It keeps me awake, aware. With a grim growl of determination, I search through my rucksack and dig out my mobile, which is running perilously low on power. I've saved the web page with Thomas Tremaine's message to me, a message disguised as a love poem. I close my eyes and brace myself. And then I shout out her name. "Morgana!"

Suddenly, she is there, in all her former glory. Tall, even more so than I used to be, with flaming hair that puts Stuart's to shame. "You little fool." She starts for me, and I have to admit, my fear puts me at a disadvantage, but I push it down, far down, only allowing myself to feel the mist against my face. "What are you *doing* here?"

"I never agreed to this, Morgana. I'm releasing us both from this deal. Now."

"Oh, really?" She shoves me, and the back of my head thunks against the stone, causing stars to start whirling around. I stagger—still all too human, me—and drop the mobile. No matter. I don't need it now.

"You thought you were being clever, didn't you?" I tell her. "Bringing us back here." The slow, burning rage building up in me has its advantages. Nothing worries me any more—what I say, Morgana's own white-hot anger. My words ring out loud and confident around us. "You made a huge mistake."

"Shut up." In one swift move, Morgana has me trapped, one hand around my neck, the other splayed against the rock, keeping her steady. "Go back to your little fiddle and do as I told you."

"No!" I've never said that to her. In fact, in all my lives, I've never said it to anyone. I begin to understand why she was never able to possess Thomas. Stubborn boy. He chose *existing*, as unsatisfying as that may have been, over a life with her. And she could never overcome that.

I think back to the scan Glen posted on the site. A smeared piece of paper, torn, almost illegible. But the verse is there, the words Thomas wanted to tell me on that fateful day. Despite the pressure of her cold fingers, I manage to choke them out,

"Cleanse me, restore me,

Make me whole…"

I say them again and again. They're soothing, not so much an indictment of Morgana as a balm for me, to strengthen my own spirit.

"Stop it!" she says. Yet, her hold grows weaker. I am able to breathe again. My gasps aren't pretty—they're strained and noisy, but they're better than the alternative. A constant, burdensome weight that had been with me for years, decades, maybe *centuries*, is gone, just like that. I feel a tingling lightness that makes me dizzy and reckless and *free*.

I push her away, but my hand seems to go through her. I feel particles, like gritty dust, but all I can see is the residue of two glowing orbs. Cold and blue. And somewhere, fading quickly, a frustrated wail of defeat.

I stumble back, my one hand still held out in front of me. And then, I'm incredibly cold and tired. All I can do is lean there, against the stone, staring, now, at nothing.

I'm not sure how much time has passed when I hear his voice, calling after me, just as he had that morning on the beach. When the old Alex died and this new one took over to destroy him.

He's suddenly beside me, the hard wind blowing his nylon jacket around him like a black parachute. "Are you trying to kill yourself? Your hair's still wet. And you hardly ever *wear* anything, Alex."

I look down. The usual uniform of thin cotton shirt and jeans. My short, sheepskin boots are the warmest articles of clothing I seem to own, and even they're more about style than substance. "Alex—" I catch myself. "This is all I packed. It's *June*. I expected it to be warmer."

"You've been to Cornwall before. You should know better." He shakes his head. "Sorry. I shouldn't scold you like that."

"I like it," I say. "It means you care."

"Too much." He lets out that funny groan again, as though he's fighting something inside him. "Here." He shrugs out of his jacket and swings it around, like a matador, so that it lands over my shoulders. "It's yours, since you're determined never to get one."

"I'm *fine!*" I try to escape from it, but he's got me by the lapels now, holding me close.

"Arms through," he says. I start to argue, but he shakes his head. "Quiet. I'm your manager. I know what's best for you. Come on, then." And I let him zip and button and tie.

"What..." I get a little lost in watching him. "What are you *doing* here?"

"My morning walk." He laughs in his self-deprecating way. "Boring old me. A creature of habit."

"I wouldn't have you any other way," I tell him.

His hands slide up, over the slippery nylon covering my arms and shoulders, and finally, after an aching time, rest against the sides of my face. And then he kisses me, sweetly and softly, just as I expected. Better than I expected. I can't help myself. I bury my own hands in his wild hair and press myself close to him. "Tom..." I whisper and that's when I realize he is separate and apart from the Thomas I knew. His own man, a man I love more than anything.

"I didn't have a chance to shave." He pulls away, rubs at his chin. "I usually...I mean, I saw you from my window and rushed out..."

I grab a handful of his shirt and yank him towards me. "I don't care," I say, and kiss him again, all over, his eyes, his delightfully scruffy cheeks, and finally, that wonderful mouth. I'm laughing and crying the whole time.

"You're mad," he says.

"I know."

A pause before he asks gently, cautiously, "Why were you running away?"

I bury my face in his neck. "I had some demons...one more demon, I had to take care of."

"And did you?"

I nod. He seems, somehow, to understand. I am reassured. I know that I will be able to tell him more. I will be able to tell him *everything*. Soon. We stand there for a while, holding each other, and I breathe him in, completely content. In none of my lives, in my never-ending existence, have I ever felt this way.

Suddenly, he disentangles his arms and reaches behind his neck. I watch, stupefied, as he takes my hand and pours the chain and medallion into it. The metal is heavy and warm against my skin. "You're the one, Alex. I want to give you this...even if you don't feel the same way."

"But I do!"

"You could have anyone. You're young, talented, *gorgeous*—"

"Really? Gorgeous?"

"A goddess," he says quietly. "And then there's me—old before my time, not in any way, shape or form a rock star..."

"Stop." I give him a quick kiss to shut him up. "I told you. I wouldn't have you any other way. I love you, Tom, so much." I rub my thumb against the textured surface of the medallion—no longer something to fear, but something to celebrate—before closing my fingers around it. "I'll treasure this."

It is time to go. As I reach down to retrieve my rucksack and mobile from the damp, mossy ground, I take a look around and bid goodbye to my dear Thomas of old. He has fulfilled his duty and set me free, so I must do the same. And Alex. I straighten and raise my hand slightly, hoping she will find ease now. "I'll make you proud," I whisper. "I promise."

Thomas touches my arm in concern, and I can't help it. I turn and hide my face in his chest so he won't see my tears. The last tears I hope to shed for a long time. And then we walk away from the Trippet Stones together, towards our future.

Timeless

The Waters of Life

Aaron K. Brookes

The Waters of Life

Finally, after five hundred years, Morny had found one. It sat in the water, gamboling with a fish or something—Morny didn't particularly care. This was her chance. The last ingredient to eternal youth was less than a hundred paces from her, and she ached to kill it, steal its blood and finish the potion. Eternal life might seem like a blessing, but in truth was a curse. Eternal youth would be the true blessing. Burentha was right about that.

Morny quietly dropped her pack on the ground and unfastened the buckles. Opening the flap, she reached inside with her withered hand and drew out the black handled knife, its hilt as long as her forearm. She took it out of the sheath, revealing the bright silver blade gleaming in the late afternoon sun. She had spent many hours polishing and sharpening this knife. A silver blade, after all, was the only way to kill a water nymph. She did not know if tarnish would affect the ability of the knife, and she was not willing to take that chance. This was the first water nymph she'd found in all these years. Morny was not willing to spend another half millennium searching for a new one because her knife had been dirty.

Morny crept down the hillside to the narrow river. She was ancient and could not move quickly, but she was also experienced and knew where to place her feet so as to not to make a sound. Her homespun gray dress fluttered in the breeze, but Morny was experienced in keeping her garments from snagging on branches. Her only desire was to take the water nymph's blood, to finish the potion. It was all she could think about.

As she neared the bank, she looked up at the creature, trying to gauge the best approach. The second she set foot in the water, it would know that she was there and she would lose her chance. She waited until the nymph began to move toward the bank, and then snuck up on it. She would cut its neck, add the blood to the potion and be gone. It wouldn't take long.

As she reached the bank, she looked down into the water. The face that looked back at her was frightening. There was little flesh left under the skin and even her wrinkles seemed to have wrinkles. Her thinning hair was stringy and white. Her once brilliant blue eyes were now faded and empty. What would it be like to regain her youth again? No matter how short the time?

She gazed at the nymph standing in front of her, only an arm-length away and raised the knife. The sight of the creature shocked her. It was a man, formed out of water. She could only see a muscled back leading to a pair of pants, also formed of water. His hair was long and literally flowed.

"Why would you want to do that?" he asked.

Morny started and backed away, hiding the knife behind her as he turned.

"Do what?" she asked, staring at his face. He looked as if he had been crafted by a master artisan, his face achieving the absolute perfection of masculine attractiveness. He appeared to be chiseled from ice, but contained a kindness and warmth that ice had never possessed. His eyes were the clear blue of the ocean that she had seen once in the far south during her travels.

"You were raising a knife towards me," he said.

"I was not. Why would you think such a thing?" Morny asked, lying with all the skill she had accumulated through the long years of her search.

"I saw you. First you looked at yourself in the pool...then you looked at me and raised the knife. You know, the one you're trying to hide behind your back?"

"How...?"

"I'm a water nymph. I can see through the reflection of the water. Really, I've had quite a few of you witches try to kill me over the years, but you're the very first who didn't know *that*."

"I'm not a witch," Morny argued.

"Why are you trying to kill me, then?"

Morny decided to drop the act. It was no use. She had failed.

"Okay, fine. I was going to kill you, but I didn't want to do it. You are such a beautiful creature."

"You desire eternal youth? I can see from your aura that you have taken the potion of Eternal Life many times and greatly extended your time in this place."

"Yes, I have, every moon for the last five hundred years."

"Even with it, though, you still age, albeit at a slower rate. You must take the potion every moon or you will die."

"You are very knowledgeable about such things," Morny answered.

The nymph laughed. "Yes, it is good to be knowledgeable about that which might bring you harm. The only ingredient you need to change your portion to the permanent potion of Eternal

Youth is the blood of a water nymph. Namely, me. I'm sorry, but I will have to disappoint you in your endeavor, my dear."

Morny began to cry. "Yes, I suspected as much."

"Come now," the water nymph told her, "there's no need to cry. I'm sure eternal youth would mean a great deal for you, but is it really worth the cost?"

"The eternal youth wasn't for me," Morny said, and at that moment one of her tears hit the water and the nymph could feel her pain.

"Oh my," he whispered. "Why don't you tell me about it?"

Morny looked at the nymph once more and his eyes were full of compassion. She dropped the knife, knowing she could never kill this wondrous creature.

"It all started almost five hundred years ago," she told him. "My fiancé was an adventurer. He and his friends hunted dangerous animals that threatened the village and even went on missions for our local lord. One day, they heard there was a woman hiring adventurers in the town's inn. They went to meet her and for some reason decided to refuse the deal." Morny sniffed.

"What happened next?"

"I'm sorry. I'm being impolite. My name is Morny."

"And mine is Mayanali. What happened next, Morny?"

She chuckled. "You are persistent. Give me a moment while I sit." The task of sitting on the ground was no longer an easy one. It felt as if every joint in her body screamed in protest, but eventually Morny was able to sit on a small rock, surrounded by the grasses that had grown high near the river. "Next, they tried to leave, but she did not want to let them go. She used powers to try to catch them, but they were young and fast. She was very old, and was only able to capture one of them. My fiancé, Essart." Morny took a deep breath.

"What kind of powers?" Mayanali asked.

"That I don't know. His friends ran away, but one of them came and told me what had happened. He would not mention what the woman did, and I could see the fear in his eyes when he even referred to it. I spent the next ten years searching for the witch, to learn the fate of my Essart. I eventually found her, twenty miles from the town I had grown up in. I asked her about Essart and she invited me in. He was there, still looking exactly the same as the last time I had seen him. The witch told me that she had placed a stasis spell over him and he would remain as he was, forever. She then seemed to think of something and told me, 'unless, of course, you were willing to do something for me.'"

"Let me guess," Mayanali interrupted. "She wanted you to collect the blood of a water nymph. What good would that do her, though? The potion would spoil within a day. Unless you were close to her home when you found one of us, it would be useless to her."

"She told me the secret to her long life and shared the potion with me so that I could search until I found a water nymph. When I found one, I was to kill it, add its blood to the potion and drink it. Then, I would return to her and she could transfer the youth to herself and set Essart free. She gave me thirteen vials of the potion, enough for one year." Morny took a deep breath, preparing to tell the rest of her story.

"Every year I return to her house and collect more potion. I have searched across this land...you are the first water nymph I have seen."

"Well, that was your first mistake. Most of my kind live in the ocean. Even now, I am only here to learn what is happening in the world of man."

Morny laughed. "It figures...all these years wasted." The laugh turned into a bitter curse. "Are all of your kind like you?" she asked.

"You mean, are there evil water nymphs that you wouldn't feel guilty about killing?"

Morny nodded, fighting a raging battle with the sorrow that threatened to consume her.

"Evil is a human frailty," Mayanali replied. "The rest of the world does what it must to survive, but it is a natural survival. Only humans attempt to break through the natural, to give themselves more than that which they could rightfully obtain."

"You mean like eternal life?"

Mayanali nodded. "Yes, that is one aspect. Although more generally, I speak of any way that a human will seek to hurt others out of greed and anger."

Morny slumped and said, "I think I see what you mean. Among your kind, there are not any who are evil because you are without greed and anger?"

"Yes," Mayanali responded.

Morny's grief, which had only threatened before, found the breach in her defenses and attacked. She slumped off the rock, sobs tearing themselves from her shriveled body. "I can't do it. I cannot rob one of you of your life. Not even to save Essart."

"Perhaps there is another way to solve this," the nymph stated. "I assume you have some of the potion with you?"

"Yes," Morny replied.

"Please get it for me."

"Hold on one moment," Morny said, slowly rose, then retraced her steps to her pack and took it to the water nymph. She withdrew one of the bottles of potion from the pack and handed it to Mayanali. As she touched its hand, she noticed that tears coursed from its pale blue eyes, down its face to drop into the water. They were barely noticeable against his watery form.

"I will need your knife as well," he said.

Morny watched as he pried the cork from the bottle, then handed him the knife. He pressed the tip of the silver blade against one of his watery fingers, then handed the knife back. She watched as a viscous green liquid slowly pooled on top of his finger—water nymph blood. He put his finger over the potion and allowed a few drops to drip into the bottle. He then corked it and shook the bottle vigorously, speaking words that Morny could not understand—words that sounded like the ocean pounding on the rocks of the shore, words that sounded like a waterfall pouring into a pool of water, and still other words that sounded like a stream tinkling through its bed.

He spoke for a long time over the bottle, always swirling it, his entire attention focused. When he finally finished, he wilted a little, as if he had expended a great deal of energy. He reached the potion toward Morny and she took it.

"The potion of Eternal Youth is finished, but I have added my own twist to it. Whoever drinks this potion will be bound to their reflection," he said.

The Waters of Life

"What does that mean?"

"Simply that whatever happens to one's reflection will happen to them, also. Do you understand what I am saying?"

Morny stared at the potion a moment, deep in thought. "Yes," she said, "I think I understand. If the reflection is destroyed, so will be the person who has drunk the potion."

"Exactly. You are wise for a human."

Morny thought he might be making a joke, but was unsure. "Drink it now," he continued, "but be sure to stay away from reflective surfaces until the witch has transferred the youth…just in case."

Morny nodded, glanced at the bottle, removed the cap and drank the potion. It felt as if her insides became liquid. She grew stronger. Her skin tightened and regained the glow of youth. She noticed her long, wispy white hair grow full and regain its color. Her joints no longer ached and the soreness that she seemed to have carried in her muscles for centuries vanished. Her first thought was to run to the stream and look at herself, but Mayanali stopped her, standing between her and the stream.

"Remember the spell that I cast upon the potion. I know it is tempting, but you must not look at yourself. It is too dangerous."

Morny nodded reluctantly. While she had never been vain, the opportunity to see herself as she had once been seemed too good to pass up, but she forced the desire down.

"You should rest now," Mayanali said. "You will want to get an early start tomorrow, I'm sure."

"Yes, of course," Morny said and tears threatened to overwhelm her again. She could finally save Essart.

"Lay here by the stream and I will watch over you tonight,"

the water nymph told her, and she thought she heard something else in his voice, too. The sound of the ocean, perhaps. She found that she did not care, all she desired was sleep. She lay near the bank, her pack next to her, and allowed her consciousness to slip off into the land of dreams.

The next morning, Morny awoke to find herself alone. She gathered her pack and began walking to the west, back to the witch's lair. She avoided human settlements. There were too many chances of her image being reflected in a mirror or a gleaming piece of metal. For the first three weeks of the journey each time she came upon a small pool of water, she wanted to go and look at her reflection, but she was able to resist the impulse.

Every step toward the witch's house made her determination not to look weaken. She yearned to see her reflection, to remember the times of her youth, before Burentha had used her foul magic on Essart. Finally, only a week from completing her journey, Morny's will crumbled as she came upon valley with a large pool surrounded by wildflowers. The sun shone brightly upon the flowers, making them appear as if they were glowing with their own radiance.

Morny crept to the pool, and warily glanced in—to find herself warily looking back. The girl in the pool had long dark hair, fair skin, and blue eyes with a nose and mouth that seemed to be in perfect proportion to the rest of her face. She was flawless. Morny had never felt this beautiful when she was young. She could always find some imperfection in her face, and she knew they were still there. After seeing herself as an aged crone for hundreds of years, however, her perspective had changed. Tears formed in her eyes and she gently reached out.

When her finger touched the water, a small ripple distorted the reflection and pain echoed through her entire body. Her face felt as if it had become liquid and rippled in sync with the water. Morny screamed—the pain was intense, worse than anything she had ever felt—and it seemed to go on forever.

After what must have been mere moments, however, the pool calmed, and her reflection stared back at her in wide-eyed horror. Morny scrambled to her feet and ran from the pool. She ran until she was gasping for air, her lungs burning and her legs aching. She fought to gain control of herself, of the panic that now coursed through her at the very thought of seeing her reflection again. When she calmed herself, she set off toward the witch's house once more, a fire lit inside her—a new determination that went beyond simply rescuing Essart—and she knew exactly what to do.

Morny steeled herself as she walked up to the witch's door, gripping the rock in the pocket of her dress once more, to reassure herself, although she had done so at least ten times. She raised her trembling hand to knock, but instead stared at it for a moment. It was the hand of a young woman, something that she would lose again in a few moments. It would have been nice to see her youthful face in a mirror one more time. To remember better times—no matter how short they had been—would have been wonderful. Only that one brief glimpse of her reflection.

Morny caught herself. This wasn't the time for regrets. There was no way to know whether seeing herself as she had been before this massive upheaval in her life would have been a moment of happiness or of gut wrenching grief. The only thing to do was move forward. Essart was on the other side of that door. She had sworn to him, and to herself, that she would save him. It was time.

The knock that reverberated from the door was strong and sure, not reflective of her brief moment of weakness and fear. The wait for Burentha to open the door seemed to take hours, although Morny knew it was only minutes. As the door creaked open, Morny heard a gasp of surprise, then a cackling laugh that nevertheless held a note of wonder in it. "You have done it," the figure sheathed in shadow rejoiced. "You have finally found a water nymph. I must say it's about time, but come in, come in."

Morny entered the witch's abode which was dimly lit by only a few sputtering candles on the mantle. The windows were sealed shut, despite the beautiful sunny day outside. She watched the witch move about the house, covered in shadow as if it were a cloak that formed itself to its wearer's shape. Morny repressed the shudder that began at the base of her spine and threatened to cause her entire body to spasm in fear. She only caught one glimpse of the witch's actual appearance. When Burentha walked in front of the two candles, the shadow cloak seemed to retreat, revealing the pure white hair of the witch. Over the years it had thinned until it now looked like strands of spider webs covering her head.

The appearance of the witch was one to inspire nightmares. Her wrinkled face appeared perfectly normal, like a great grandmother. What was not normal was the malice that shone from that gaze. Her hazel eyes sparkled with a hate that was not focused on Morny, but rather the entire world. As the witch stepped back into the shadow, having gathered a tool from the mantle, Morny saw the darkness engulf her hair and face once more, except for the eyes. The witch's eyes, which were now peering in her direction shone menacingly yellow, like a cat at night that had spotted its prey.

"It is good that you have finally returned with the potion. I have been cleaning out my stores, and I am running out of room. I was thinking of getting rid of my favorite statue before much longer." Burentha cackled hysterically.

Morny followed the witch's pointing finger—at least she assumed it must be her finger, as making out anything about the witch's form in the dark was impossible—to find Essart in the same place she had last seen him, stuffed between two cabinets. He was covered in dust and cobwebs, his expression frozen in the same mask of shock as she had seen all the hundreds of times she had been to the witch's house. Morny ran to him and began brushing the dust from his face, the cobwebs from his hair. She gazed into his dark brown eyes—as she always did—but could see no sign that he was there.

At that moment, Morny heard the witch begin to chant. Strange symbols lit up around the room, on the floor, ceiling, and all four walls, in a reddish light that reminded Morny of blood.

"Come, my dear," Burentha said. "Let's transfer the enchantment and then I'll set him free."

With that, Morny played her card. Drawing the silver knife from her sleeve, she held the tip near her heart, placed where it would miss her ribs and puncture her life.

"Time for a change of plans, Burentha," Morny announced, her voice shaking in fear at what she was doing. Her hand, however, was rock steady on the end of the knife.

"What do you think you're going to do, girl?" the witch said, sneering. "Have me wake him and then the two of you escape? I would rather you both die, and I spend another thousand years looking for my youth."

"I will give you your youth, Burentha, but I don't trust you to live up to your side of the bargain. So we're going to do this my way. First, you wake up Essart, and then I will give you what you want."

Burentha seemed to mull this over. Probably thinking of any way Morny could try to trick her. Morny, on the other hand, had no illusions that she could trick the witch and get away with it. The only play was to give the witch what she wanted, but Essart had to be freed first.

After a few moments, Burentha pointed at the door and muttered some words in a language that Morny had never heard, then turned to face Morny once more. "Very well, my dear. We shall do this your way, but there is no escape from this house if your goal is trickery."

Morny simply nodded and gestured at Essart. Burentha continued to gaze in her direction. Morny couldn't see the witch's eyes, but she assumed that they were calculating, trying to figure out what Morny's motives were. At the same time, Morny knew—given the witch's past dealings—Burentha herself would always demand to have her side of the deal fulfilled first, so Morny's request fit in with her worldview. Morny finally decided that Burentha mostly didn't like giving up her advantage before getting what she wanted.

Burentha walked over to a cabinet and began rummaging inside. Morny didn't know how the witch could see anything in the faint light given off by the two candles. Burentha turned from the cabinet and walked to her worktable in the middle of the room, pouring powders together inside of a mortar, then grinding them together with a pestle. She added water to the mixture, and a few other things that were probably best not to know, before adding the mixture to two cups and chanting over them.

Morny stood by Essart's side the entire time, watching as the witch chanted. It went on for hours and as Burentha chanted, the color of the potion in the cups began to change. At first they had simply been a dark color that Morny could not make out in the already dim room. Then they began to glow a dark purple color, the luminescence so faint that Morny thought she imagined it. Eventually the dark purple turned into a pale purple, then a blue like a river on summer day. Finally the potions glowed a pale blue, like the southern seas. The light from the potions was much brighter than that of the two candles, and where Morny had seen only shadows, now they were pushed back, revealing more of the room's contents.

The walls were cluttered with closets, chests, and tables for the witch's paraphernalia. The only places that were different was the space where the door was to the outside, another doorway that led further into the house, the fireplace, and, sure enough, a mirror. It was covered with a black cloth, to prevent the witch from having to gaze upon herself, but Morny had assumed correctly that Burentha would be prepared to gain her youth once more.

After a while, Morny's legs began to hurt from standing still for so long, but she did not move. She watched the witch chant, ready to plunge the knife into her chest if she tried anything. Finally, after hours, it ended. The pale blue potion continued to light the room.

"It is done," the witch said.

"The potion will cure Essart?" Morny asked. "How will we

get him to drink it?"

"Of course the potion won't cure the boy, you silly girl. It is the potion that will give me your youth."

"We had a deal. Essart first," Morny cried, preparing to thrust the knife into her own chest.

"Yes, girl, we have a deal, but as you have seen, this potion took quite a while to make, and I would not risk you and the boy trying to harm me or escape while my attention was diverted." With that, Burentha turned to Essart and muttered three words. His arm, which had been frozen for the last five hundred years at a slight angle as if beginning to reach out, fell to his side and twitched. He breathed in a ragged breath and slumped onto the cabinet next to him.

"Wha...what happened?" he finally managed, pushing himself upright and looking around the room. "Where am I?"

Morny watched as his roaming gaze settled on the witch. He gasped, started to say something, and then he noticed her standing there. His eyes lit up when he saw her, but confusion quickly took over again. "Morny, what are you doing? Why are you here?"

"It's okay, Essart. It's a long story. We can talk about it later."

"Yes," Burentha interrupted. "That *is* something you can discuss later. You have a bargain to maintain, girl. I have restored him. Now you have to pay up."

Morny took one more look at Essart and said, "Please, remember me as I am now, my love. Not as I will be."

"What is going on here?" he asked. "Morny, whatever you're doing, you don't have to."

"I'm afraid I do, Essart. I made an agreement, and I will live up to it."

"Very good, very good," Burentha said, walking toward Morny with one of the cups of potion. "Drink this, and then you will be free to go."

Essart reached forth and grabbed the witch's hand. "She will not drink it," he growled.

Morny took Essart's hand and gently pried it free of Burentha's.

"I do what I must, my love. You cannot change this. Do not try."

A pained expression crossed his face. He didn't know what was about to happen, but apparently he had figured out that it wouldn't be good for Morny. She chose to ignore it, though she felt her heart ripping in half. She did not want to cause him pain, especially when he found out that she would only live for a few more moons. There was nothing to be done about it now, though. She took the potion from the witch's hand. Burentha walked back to the work table to get the other potion, a spring in her step that had not been there before, as if she could already feel the youth flooding into her veins.

"Now drink, girl, drink it all," Burentha exclaimed, glee pouring forth from her in both words and actions. Her wrinkled, ragged face had softened in the pale blue light from the potion as hope replaced her normal, evil glare. She now truly looked like a kindly great-grandmother. Morny found that to be the most disconcerting.

Morny lifted the cup to her mouth, fearing the loss of her youth that she had already lost once in her mad search for the megalomaniacal witch, fearing the look on Essart's face when he saw her as she had been—a woman who looked half way into the grave. A small part of her dreaded the taste of the brew—some of the things the witch had added together had looked entirely unwholesome. Morny ignored these distractions, for that was all they were, and forced herself to drink the potion. It had no taste. It was much like drinking water, and she downed the entire potion quickly. She just wanted this over.

Burentha had also finished her potion and they stared at each other as they lowered their glasses. The room returned to the pale lighting of the two dim candles. Despite this, Morny could still see the witch's eyes glowing with satisfaction and anticipation. It took a few moments, but then Morny began to feel it. The room became even darker than it had been. Her eyesight lost the precision of youth and her strength faded. She could feel the weight of her body once more, dragging upon her. Her skin dried up and a tingling sensation told Morny that her body was being laced through with wrinkles. From the edge of her vision, she could see a lock of her dark hair fade to gray, then to white.

Her gaze, however, remained locked on the witch. Burentha's posture slowly straightened as the witch stood to her full height for the first time in a millennium. Morny could not see much of the witch's face in the shadow, but her skin seemed to be smoothing and the patchy white hair on the top of the witch's head became full. Color seemed to flood into the hair, starting at the roots, a pale blonde color that was appealing. When Morny could no longer feel herself changing, Burentha laughed in delight, threw up her hands and shouted another word from the strange language she had used when incanting the spell.

A bright light filled the room and Morny got a good look at the witch. She was absolutely perfect, the most beautiful woman Morny had ever seen. Her figure was impressive and her face was so beautiful that any man would stop and stare in awe. It was an example of such perfection that many women would probably stop as well, with envy clawing out their insides.

Morny, however, did not feel envy. She felt only hate. This was the second time the witch had stolen her youth from her. True, she had gotten to live out her youth the first time, but it had been spent searching for the witch and then for the water nymph. Burentha had taken everything from her, and soon Morny would die. She had sacrificed her life for Burentha to achieve this moment.

Involuntarily Morny's gaze moved to Essart. Tears filled his eyes when he looked at her. She tried to pull her gaze from his, fearing the look of revulsion that she knew would soon replace his wide eyed look of fear, but she could not look away. Panic coursed through Morny's body as she watched Essart's expression begin to change.

The revolted look that Morny feared did not come to pass. Instead, Essart's fear was replaced with the look of love that had always resided on his expression when he looked at her. Morny felt her heart melt and her strength finally failed her. She stumbled and almost fell, but Essart darted forward and caught her. Morny could not draw her gaze away from his face, or the love that she saw there.

At least not until she sensed Burentha moving across the room. Morny focused on her once more, just as the witch ripped the shroud from the mirror in the room. It was a full length mirror on a wooden stand. Burentha laughed in delight when she saw her reflection. "At long last," she said, her gaze never leaving her image.

"I became a witch for this, you know. To preserve this beauty. It took me years to learn what I needed to extend my life and many more years to discover how to regain my youth, but at last, I am young again."

Morny leaned into Essart and reached into her pocket, withdrawing the fist-sized stone. She searched for Essart's hand while never looking away from the witch. Upon finding him, Morny pressed the stone into his fist, and finally broke her gaze from the witch to look at him.

"The mirror," she whispered. "Break the mirror."

Essart looked confused for a moment, but then nodded. Morny watched Burentha from the corner of her eye while the witch continued to admire herself, but also saw Essart draw the rock back, and then hurl it at the mirror.

Time seemed to slow when the mirror shattered into numerous pieces. The remnants of the silvery glass fell to the floor. Burentha screamed and cracks seemed to form throughout her body as she stared at the broken mirror.

"What is this?" she screeched. "What have you done?"

The look of terror on her face clutched at Morny's heart, despite all that the witch had put her through. At that moment, the pain must have become too much, as Burentha lost control of her spell to light the room. When the light faded, Burentha disappeared, like a reflection disappearing from a mirror in the darkness.

Morny exhaled a breath that she had not realized she was holding. She looked at Essart, and then walked over to the mirror. The witch's clothes were piled on the floor, the water nymph's spell only affecting whoever had benefitted from the potion and not their clothing.

"What...happened?" Essart asked.

"The youth potion that I drank had a spell on it. When the mirror was cracked and destroyed, so was she, and when the light went out and the reflection disappeared, she winked out of existence also."

"I wonder what would have happened had there still been light for the reflection?"

"I don't know," Morny replied. "I think that she was holding herself together with magic, but there was no way to repair the damage. She would have eventually died no matter what."

They continued to stare at the room for long moments, unable to break free of everything that had happened. Finally, Morny shuffled over to one of the bookshelves next to a table by the wooden wall. She grabbed books and scrolls and piled them onto the table, opening the books and unrolling the scrolls. Eventually, Essart joined her with a quizzical look, but did not ask what they were doing. When Morny judged that the pile of paper on the desk was arranged to her satisfaction, she slowly walked to the counter, her joints protesting movement of any kind, and picked up one of the sputtering candles.

As she walked back to the table with the pile of books and parchment, she thought of how much trouble this place had caused her and Essart. If it hadn't been for Burentha, they would have grown old together and died a long time ago, but it would have been worth it. She couldn't help thinking that her life had been stolen from her. Upon reaching the table, she looked around the shadowy room once more.

"Essart, would you mind grabbing my pack?" she asked, and then a thought struck her. "Oh, and make sure the door will open."

Essart scooped her pack up from the floor by the door and tried pulling the handle. The door opened quietly. Whatever force Burentha had used to seal it was no longer active. Morny lit the various books and parchment in a few places, feeling a twinge of guilt at burning them, but also realizing that the knowledge should not be passed on. The aged parchment caught quickly and soon fire engulfed the table.

Morny felt Essart tugging her arm gently. "It's time to go, love," he told her. "Just let it go."

Morny nodded and followed him out the door. She began walking back to her home, the place she had once planned to raise a family with Essart, and felt tears slipping down her cheeks. Essart looked at her, put his arm around her shoulder and helped her along.

"If you're up for it, could you tell me what's happened, Morny?" he asked.

Morny fought to pull herself together. Yes, he would be curious about what had transpired. As they walked, she told him, haltingly at first, the entire tale, from his capture by the witch to Mayanali's plan to stop Burentha. It took her two days to tell everything she could think of from the past five hundred years. It also took two days to cover the twenty miles to town, with barely any rest. Morny tried to keep the bitterness from her voice, but she knew she often failed. She had two, maybe three months left to live.

"You keep saying that our life together has been stolen from us," Essart said.

"It has been," Morny replied. "Burentha took everything from me."

"Not everything, Morny. You saved me and you have me back now. No matter how short our time together will be, we have each other. You cannot focus on what you have lost and what is in the past, or your life truly will be stolen. You have to live in the present and enjoy the life that you have. Then you will have truly defeated the witch."

Morny stared at Essart. She had forgotten just how wise he could be. "You're right. I need to focus on the time I have left."

She allowed the thought of her remaining time with Essart to warm her. True, she was insecure about the fact that she was so very old while he was a young man, but she could see the way he looked at her, as if she were the only thing in the world. When she had told her story, that look had only grown stronger, his admiration of her deeper. There wasn't much time left to be together, but she had spent her entire life trying to free him, and she forced herself to rejoice in this time that she now had. She found it bittersweet.

When they entered the town, Morny noticed little, although Essart couldn't get over the changes since he had last been here. He kept asking her about them, but received little response. She didn't know what to tell him. She had been through here often in the last five hundred years, and it was constantly in a state of flux. When they had spent their innocent youths here, it had been a small mining town. The mines had been rich and the town had grown until they ran dry four hundred years ago. It had then shrunk considerably until about one hundred years ago when it had become a major trading post between the capital and the new frontier cities in the north.

Now the town boasted four inns. Morny chose one of the nicer ones. It was a three story building in good repair. The downstairs was filled with tables that were crowded with merchants and local guards. Upon asking for one room, the innkeeper gave them a strange look, shook his head and went back to wiping down his bar. Morny felt a sharp stab of embarrassment, and fled up the stairs as quickly as she could.

The room was small with one bed—which made Morny blush—a small table, and a washstand. The smell of the fresh flowers on the table and the freshly laundered sheets could not completely mask the scent of unwashed bodies. Morny placed her pack on the table, then doubled over in pain as an ache began through her midsection and worked its way through her whole body.

"Morny," she faintly heard Essart yell.

He helped her to sit on the bed, where she curled up in a ball, clenching her teeth against the pain to keep from screaming in agony. Essart hovered over her, and through the tears in her eyes, Morny could see that he was confused, worried, and had no idea what to do.

"My bag," she managed to murmur before another wave of pain wracked her body. It seemed to take forever for Essart to cross the room, grab her bag and bring it back—a journey of no more than three steps. He placed the pack on the bed next to her and opened it, looking at the contents as if the one she needed would jump to the top and yell, "Pick me."

The pain finally subsided enough for her to grab the bag herself and begin rummaging around through it, searching for the potion.

"What's wrong, Morny? What's happening?" Essart's voice shook in what Morny assumed to be terror. She didn't bother looking at him, she didn't have time.

"It's the potion wearing off," Morny panted. "I thought I would have more time than this. It's one more month that witch has stolen from me."

Morny gently began to sob. She finally found her last two bottles of potion tucked into the bottom corner of her pack. Two more moons of life and then this night would be repeated, with no way to stop the inevitable. She tried to tug one of the bottles from the pack, but it seemed to be stuck and she was unable to remove it. Essart, seeing what she was reaching for gently removed her weakened hands from the pack and carefully pulled out both bottles. The reason Morny had been unable to pull out the bottle she desired seemed to be because they were both tied together with reeds.

"That's not how I put them in there," she said, as a small wave of pain rippled through her.

"There's a note attached," Essart said. He drew his knife and began to carefully cut away the reeds. When he had freed the bottles, he handed the note to Morny.

She unfolded the delicate parchment and read the note. "That which is freely given is much more powerful than that which is taken by force. I have added the tears I shed at the telling of your tale to these potions. One is for you, the other for your love. Drink them."

Morny dropped the note as its implications hit her. Essart pried the top off of one of the bottles and handed it to her, but she simply stared at it for long moments.

"What's wrong with you, Morny? Drink the potion," Essart told her.

"It's not the potion I thought it was, Essart. The water nymph I told you about has changed it from the Potion of Eternal Life to the Potion of Eternal Youth. If I drink this, I will live forever, as young as I was the other day."

"What's the problem then? Drink it. I can't bear losing you, Morny."

"Mayanali gave me one for you, also," she said, nodding at the remaining bottle he held. "I cannot drink this unless you drink yours. I will not spend eternity without you."

He looked at her, his gaze full of love. "An eternity with you sounds like a dream come true…finally," he whispered.

Essart removed the lid from his own bottle and drank the potion, but nothing happened. "I don't feel any different, did you see any change?" he asked.

"Of course not, silly. You are already young. it wouldn't change your current appearance."

Morny looked at the potion and thought of all the trouble it had brought her. If it wasn't for this potion, she would have never lost Essart in the first place. She would not have spent her youth searching out the witch. She would not have had to wander the world for five centuries, searching for the key ingredient.

"Morny, aren't you going to drink it?" Essart asked, his voice high-pitched as if he were about to panic.

Morny looked up from the potion at Essart. Without this potion she would never have seen the wonders she had seen, met Mayanali, or be able to spend eternity with her love.

"I was just reminiscing, Essart. We elderly are prone to that from time to time." She smiled.

Essart snorted, which earned him a dirty look from Morny. She shook her head, muttered, "young people," and drank the potion. Once again her skin prickled as it tightened across her body. She felt her bones growing stronger, along with her muscles, her eyesight became sharper, and her hearing better. She looked at Essart and saw the huge smile playing across his mouth.

Morny harrumphed. "I see you enjoy my looking like this better than the other way."

Essart laughed and shook his head. "No, my dear, you were beautiful to me either way, because you were still Morny. I would spend eternity with you as a young maiden or as a dignified grandmother... I'm just glad to have more than a few months left with you."

With that, he leaned down and kissed her. It was a passionate kiss, full of wonder and excitement, the perfect representation of what they were both feeling. Morny began to feel lightheaded and pushed him away. He looked a bit shocked that she had pushed him away, and a bit in awe at the kiss.

Morny couldn't contain herself, and a small giggle burst from her lips. "Yes, you're right. We had our lives stolen from us by Burentha and now they are restored to us by Mayanali. I have something I have to do." She rose from the bed. She couldn't stop herself from throwing her arms around him and giving him one more kiss that left them both panting for breath by the time she pulled away.

She walked to the washstand and poured the water from the pitcher into the bowl, then stared at it, unsure how to achieve her goal—or if it was even possible. She felt Essart walk up behind her and place his hand on her shoulder as he also gazed into the bowl. She finally decided that the best she could do was try.

"Mayanali," she told the water, "everything worked according to plan. Burentha is dead and Essart and I have taken the potions. I don't know how I can ever thank you for everything you have done for us, but my eternal gratitude is yours."

A gentle ripple disturbed the surface of the water.

The Sun and the Star

Elyse Salpeter

The Sun and the Star

1912 Kansas

An October dusk settled over the hundreds of rows of withered corn stalks standing like sentries in the Kansas field. The full moon was rising and a brisk wind whistled through the dry shoots, creating a noise like paper crinkling, and drowning out the sounds of the young girl crying.

No one was working in the field that day. It was Sunday, the one day I gave my farmhands off. My own homestead was but a few trots down the road on the only hill this side of Kansas, but everyone in any direction could see we were home that evening from the smoke swirling from the chimney. I always wondered what the girl did that long cold night while my family and I slept. Wondered why she didn't come and seek our help.

We wouldn't find her until late the next afternoon when the workers had returned to pull the stalks and ready the field for winter. I remember exactly where I was when they found her.

"Boss, help!" The farmhand ran out from one of the rows frantically, carelessly stomping through the dead plants. If it were summer, I would have docked his pay for doing something so flagrant, but I knew this man. He was a good worker and was a family man. It must be bad.

I rode up on my horse. "Langston, what's the problem?"

He leaned over, his hands on his knees, wheezing and trying to catch his breath. I stood up on the stirrups, able to peer over the stalks and saw a group of my men converging in an area about a quarter mile down the rows. Great, it was probably a cow from the McKensey farm next door that had wandered over and died in my field. It had happened before.

Langston stood up, huffing. "Boss, we found a little girl."

Dread ran through me. "Is she dead?"

He shook his head. "No, she isn't, but she's sick. We gotta get help."

I yelled at my foreman to run to my house and call for my wife and then jumped off the horse and raced with Langston through the rows toward the child. Thoughts competed in my head. Why would a little girl be here? Did someone hurt her? Did an animal drag her here? Images of my own three children coursed through my brain and made me run faster, but when I pulled into the clearing the men had created, everything I expected was shattered.

This wasn't a toddler. It was a young girl of about fifteen, curled into a ball and lying in the dirt in the middle of my cornfield. Strangely twisted and charred hunks of metal smoked in the field around her, creating a clearing. The air reeked of scorched corn and burnt oil, and as I stared at the boulder sized lumps glowing red-hot in places, they reminded me of the color of the branding irons we used on the bulls in stock.

The men squirmed nervously. "Extraterrestre," they mumbled. You could practically smell their fear.

"Don't be ridiculous. It's just a child, nothing more," I admonished, trying to convince myself as well.

I leaned down next to the girl, her long white-blonde hair covering her face. Pushing the locks away from her forehead, she turned her ice blue eyes to mine and something in her stare shook me to my very core. To this day, I couldn't tell you exactly what it was about her, but it was something. Her face was heart-shaped, her features petite and mystically beautiful, but she was hurt. Bruises covered her forehead, cheeks and arms, her plain white dress was filthy from ash and dirt and there were blisters forming from burns on her bare legs. The child craned her head to the sky and you could see little tattoos of stars and musical notes scattered on her neck, directly under her right ear. Her eyes bubbled with tears as she stared at the rising moon. She seemed so lost, so terribly alone. I tried to take her hand, but she clutched a strange instrument to her chest and refused to let it go. They told me later it was a musical instrument, resembling an ancient Greek lyre. To me it just looked like a small harp. Instead, I patted her hand, surprised at how warm it was and thought she might have a fever.

"It's okay, miss. We'll get you out of here. Langston, have one of your men hook up the wagon." I picked up the girl, contraption and all, and cradled her in my arms. She was but a doll, so slight. As we moved to the main road, she made the slightest of noises in her throat, but I couldn't tell what she was saying. In fact, no one could.

We brought the girl to the local hospital but no one could identify her. She talked gibberish, crying and sobbing incessantly, humming haunting melodies and playing her instrument. But every few minutes she tried to get to the window to look out, always trying to look outside and stare at the sky. The staff was so concerned she was going to jump, they moved her to the psychiatric ward and that's the last I ever heard of her.

As for the charred chunks of metal? By the time we got back to the field to remove them for plowing, the strange stuff had burned itself away. Except for some blackened ash, I wondered if it had been there at all.

2012 New York City

It was an unusually cold October evening in New York City, the last of the late night restaurants closing their doors for the day. The taxis seemed to be the only cars on the street, whisking passengers to all ends of the boroughs. This time of night was when the real New York could be seen. The homeless coming out of their cellars and subways, able to walk the streets without being harassed, rummaging through garbage cans for food along with the other crazy folks who'd been turned out of mental hospitals because of overcrowding. And then there were the children. Teenagers who society seemed to have forgotten and who milled together in groups for safety, hopping from bus and train depots to vacant buildings, trying to find refuge for the night.

In the middle of the city was an enormous park called Central Park. Inside were tons of hidden crevices, old structures, and underground passages. If you knew where to look you could find any number of places to hide, safe from the elements and from those insane and murderous individuals who made evening their hunting time. In the midst of the park was an ornate stone public bathroom facility. Two teenagers crowded together on the floor inside the women's stalls, the lock the Park Security used each night to secure the door, picked and lying discarded on the chipped tiles beside them.

"Where is she?" The speaker was male, deeply tattooed and very thin. A coarse, dark stubble stood out on his pale chin and cheeks. Sixteen years old and scarred from years of abuse, he'd left home at the age of thirteen and had lived on the streets ever since.

"Jacob, Kira will be here soon. She's getting dinner," said a young girl, calmly. Fourteen and much too curvy for her age, her afro haloed like a giant dome around her face. She rubbed her bare arms, shivering slightly, and took out a frayed jacket from her backpack.

A noise sounded outside and the door squeaked open. The very air seemed to warm up as a girl of fifteen came in, a worn and scuffed lyre strapped to her back and loaded down with bags. "I'm here already and if you're both trying to be quiet, you're doing a horrible job. I could hear you babbling all the way across the square." She tossed Jacob a bag filled with fresh bagels and rolls she'd gotten from one of the local delis. Another bag she gave to Monique, heavy with cartons of milk, bags of chips and a handful of apples.

"Excellent!" Jacob said, ferociously tearing into a bagel.

Kira sat down next to them, placing her cherished instrument gently at her side and tossing back her white-blonde braids. You could see tattoos of a musical note and stars under her right ear. Her jeans were torn and her fingernails were dirty, but she was still strikingly beautiful. With blue eyes, a button nose and a delicate frame, people who listened to her play sometimes wondered who she was and what had happened for her to become homeless. Very few people walked by her without dropping at least a few pieces of change into her cup.

"I played all day at the bus depot and made a lot today." She threw the rest of her money in the baseball cap lying on the floor. Monique and Jacob rifled through their pockets and deposited what they made begging as well.

Jacob nodded. "Twenty-six dollars. You know, we have enough to go downtown and rent a room at Delila's for the night."

Monique wrinkled her nose. "I don't like that place. All those crazy people always getting in our business."

Kira nodded. "Yeah, but at least we'd be able to shower and sleep in a real bed." Kira stood up and crossed to the window, staring at the sky longingly.

"What is it with you and full moons, Kira?" Monique asked, chugging from a carton of milk.

Kira turned to her, her face wistful. "They remind me of a fairytale I heard once when I was a little girl. It's an old story…" Her voice trailed off.

"How old?" Monique asked. She shivered again and rubbed her fingers together to get them warm.

Kira sighed. "Older than you."

Jacob grabbed the milk from Monique and took a swig. Wiping his mouth on his sleeve, he nodded at Kira. "Well, you might as well tell us, we're not going anywhere. And will you come over and sit next to Monique already and get her warm? You're the hottest chick I know, and I don't mean cute."

Kira grinned and sat down next to Monique, but not before punching Jacob playfully in the arm. Then she took Monique's hands in hers and rubbed them together. Within seconds Monique's fingers warmed up.

Monique flexed her hands. "You're a radiator, girl. It's crazy, like you always have a fever or something."

"Lucky me," Kira mused. She picked up a bagel and took a tentative bite. Swallowing, she started speaking.

"Once upon a time, in a land far, far away, there was a boy and girl and they were deeply in love."

Jacob rolled his eyes. "Are you seriously going to tell us a love story?"

Kira nodded, grinning slightly. "Yes, but I promise you won't be disappointed."

With that she closed her eyes and started talking and soon both of the other children forgot they were sitting in an empty cold bathroom in the middle of Central Park and were soon deep in the foreign land of Xetathana.

1912 in the Xetathana Castle Gardens

The two teenagers walked amidst the purple flowers in the back castle gardens of Xetathana, strolling through a part of the grounds the gardeners let grow more rampant and wild. Flowers spread in wild abandon amidst water gardens and gurgling fountains. Tendrils of red and green vines stretched from tree to tree, blooming with rose-colored blooms that hung down in hundreds of cascading sprays. Under one of the more profuse canopies, the boy took the girl's hand and sat her down on the perfumed grass. The moons were full tonight, lighting up the sky with their three huge orbs, and the teens stared at them and held hands, watching them lazily drift across the heavens. Every now and then a rocket launched, creating fiery trails that lit up the night like fireworks. The boy leaned over and gave the girl a tentative kiss on the lips.

"I love you, Kyralee. I want to be with you forever."

She touched his cheek and stared deeply into his brilliant green eyes. "It can never be, Phasha. Your parents won't allow it. The kingdom would never allow it."

He pushed aside her beautiful long white-blonde hair, revealing the star and musical note tattoos she'd been given at birth. The one showing her family's status as musicians and entertainers. Levels removed from his position in the kingdom as the first son of the King and Queen of Xetathana.

She ran her own hands down his chin, tracing her fingers along his own tattoo of a brilliant sun and moon on his neck.

Phasha gripped her hand, his voice angry. "We'll run away together."

Kyralee shook her head. "We'll be punished. We'll be killed. It's happened before."

"They won't find us, Kyralee. We'll hide away with the tree and grass people and then flee to the mountains and live with the strange wood folk. I have money, goods, and we'll take our horses. Please. Meet me tomorrow outside the gardens at midnight and we'll just disappear. I promise I'll take care of you. We can do this."

Kyralee peered longingly in his eyes, wanting so desperately to believe him.

He smiled and it was as if the world stood still. She could deny this boy nothing when he smiled at her.

Phasha grinned triumphantly. He knew he'd won. Standing, he pulled Kyralee to her feet.

She took the instrument she had brought with her this evening and strummed a haunting cord, the melody so beautiful that within seconds Phasha was mesmerized. She watched as his eyes slowly closed, his breathing calm, knowing in just moments she could put him into a deep, blissful sleep. She ceased playing, letting him come back to himself, knowing he'd be happy and content for hours.

Shaking his head as if waking from a dream, he walked with her to the edge of the castle gardens and pushed aside some ivy on the stone wall, revealing a key panel. He typed in the code and a door opened in the wall that led into the forest. Kyralee's own filly neighed quietly nearby and they moved towards her. Kyralee put her instrument's strap around her shoulder and then jumped on, taking the reins.

She leaned down and kissed her beloved lightly on the lips.

"I will be here, Phasha. Tomorrow at midnight."

"As will I." He patted Kyralee's horse on the rump and they took off, trotting through the forest. He listened until he could hear no more and then returned to the castle.

The next evening at midnight, with the moons still full, Kyralee showed up at the back of the gardens. As she jumped off her horse and moved to punch the code for the door, she was suddenly surrounded by the castle guard who grabbed her and pulled her back. Her shrieks riddled the air. Phasha came tearing through the forest on his steed, screaming at his men to leave her alone. He jumped down and flew to her side.

"Don't touch her!" he yelled, shielding her with his body as Kyralee cowered behind him.

An ominous voice sounded from the forest and Phasha turned. "No, you don't touch her!" It was the King emerging from the dense trees and riding a massive robotic creature with Kyralee's father chained to a similar mechanical beast beside him, his neck shackles glowing a bright yellow.

"Father!" Kyralee cried, trying to run to him, but the guards held her back.

The king ignored her, his eyes on his son. "How dare you go against me?" His voice boomed. "You know her position and yours. You know your responsibilities. A note and star are not meant for you, Phasha! You're to be a king. We told you this will never work, told you the consequences if you continued to see this girl. Now that you both intend to flee, you've given us no choice."

Kyralee's father spoke up. "What will you do with her? You can't kill her just because she loves your son!" The neck shackles tightened and now blazed a bright red. Kyralee's father grimaced in pain.

The King turned to him, his face indignant. "You best calm yourself down if you don't want to choke to death. I have no intention of killing her, but something will be done. Bring her to transport."

Phasha's eyes bulged in comprehension. "Father, no! You can't do this to her! To me!" He grabbed for Kyralee, but the guards picked her up and they took to their mechanized steeds, in seconds racing to the docking stations.

Riding through the village, the screams of Kyralee and Phasha waking everyone, townspeople followed until there were hundreds of inhabitants of Xetathana surrounding the transport docking station, an open field filled with black space pods atop square launch platforms, waiting to deploy.

"Father, please don't do this!" Phasha cried, as they pushed and pulled Kyralee, screaming and fighting, up one of the platforms and into a pod, securing her to the seat. Phasha tried to stop them, but was thrown back to the ground by the castle guards and held there, unable to get to her. Within seconds she was locked in.

"Phasha, help me!" she beseeched. The guards slammed the door, drowning out her cries. A heavy mist began to fill the inside of the pod unit.

Phasha threw off the guards and ran up to the spaceship, staring through the window, punching at the glass, watching helplessly as Kyralee disappeared into the fog. "Father, you can't do this!" He raced back down the steps and to the control station on the ground, but the guards held him back.

Phasha flinched as the engines started.

The king glared at him, his face stony. "I can't? You've given me no choice. I told you months ago what would happen if you chose a note and star over the sun and moon. The girl will be sent to Earth for a period of a hundred years as punishment for going against our ways."

The crowd gasped.

"King, I beg of you. She's my only daughter," Kyralee's father said. Tears streaked his cheeks. "I'll take her away to the mountains. Away from the castle. I promise you she'll never set foot in the kingdom again. Will never see Phasha again. Please."

The king turned to him. "It's too late for that. You should have taught her our ways better, made her understand the consequences. Be lucky, minstrel. I could have had her destroyed." With that he turned to his men. "Send it off."

The engines came full throttle, fire and plumes of smoke erupting on the dock and the villagers all raced back, away from the searing heat. The pod shook and lifted to the sky.

"No!" Phasha cried, falling to his knees as the ship shot into the atmosphere. In seconds it disappeared from view, streaking across the universe towards the Milky Way Galaxy.

Phasha turned to his father, his face a mask of hate and disgust. "I will never forgive you for this."

The king huffed. "One day you'll thank me. For now you can give your mother the credit for this most compassionate of punishments. I personally would have chosen a different, more permanent penalty." The king turned his face to the townspeople who had gathered. A mix of suns, stars, moons, musical notes and a smattering of trees, grass, flowers, hammers and planets who ventured to watch the punishment given to one of their own.

The king addressed the villagers. "For going against the kingdom rules, for disobeying our customs, the girl will be dealt with in the most humane of ways. The atmosphere on Earth will keep her unmarred and she will not age. When she returns to Xetathana, she will be as if she never left."

Phasha glared at him. "How can you say that? She'll be a hundred and fifteen years old in a fifteen-year old body! Everything will be different. Everyone she knows will be dead. I'll be dead!"

The king stared down at Phasha from his horse. "But she'll be alive. And for that, you should be eternally grateful, son." He nodded towards Kyralee's father. "Unlock him."

The guards unlocked the chains around Kyralee's father's wrists and neck and he dropped to the ground, shaking. The king shook his head in disgust, called for his guards and they left the docking station, leaving Phasha on his knees in the dirt, sobbing quietly.

Kyralee's father moved to the boy's side and bent down to him.

"I'm so sorry, sir," said the boy. "I'm so very sorry."

The man patted his back, tentatively. "Prince, a sun and moon has no business with a note and star. You both knew that."

The boy looked up at the man and shook his head. "It's not true." Phasha stood and turned his head to the sky, staring at the moons. "I promise I'll come for you, Kyralee. Wait for me," he whispered. Sadly, he bent his head and dejectedly walked the five miles back to the kingdom.

Kira stopped talking and stared at the two teens listening enthralled as they sat on the bathroom floor. Their breath steamed in the cold night air, but no one noticed.

"So what happened?" Monique asked, eagerly. "Did they return for her? What happened when she went home? Was the boy even alive?"

Kira shook her head and shrugged. "I don't know."

Jacob's jaw dropped. "What do you mean you don't know? How do you not know the ending?"

Kira stood and walked back over to the window, looking up at the full moon. "Because the story isn't over yet. But it will be soon." She quickly moved to her lyre and before her friends could say anything, she began to play a haunting melody. Her fingers moved ferociously, the pace getting faster and faster as the notes rose and fell. This was no endearing little tune to entice people to leave her some coins, no pop cover song for them to skip or hum along to while on their commute. This tune was altogether alien, unfamiliar and foreign and her friends had never heard her play like this before with such abandonment and passion. Without their knowing what was happening, they became transfixed, mesmerized.

Kira watched them carefully as she played. Watched as the stubble on Jacob's face began to slowly fade and disappear, watched as he seemed to shrink an inch, then two. Watched as Monique's face and body changed from being on the cusp of womanhood to that of a young girl. Her body became softer, her eyes wider. Both children tottered where they sat and suddenly fell to the ground, unconscious.

Kira ceased playing, and stepped over to them, touching Jacob's cheek. It was now silky smooth, the face of a twelve year old before puberty had hit him. She turned to Monique, now like a baby. She seemed no older than ten.

"I'm so sorry," Kira whispered. How many individuals did she say those very words to in the past hundred years? How many people did she have to leave because she couldn't spend too much time with them or they'd simply disappear into youth?

She took her lyre and left the bathroom, walking to the middle of the Great Lawn, an open area in Central Park so large the city used it for concerts and big events. As Kira stood in the middle of the deserted field, searching the stars, she found the point in the sky where her galaxy was, and felt a lump form in her throat. She knew nothing would ever be the same again.

A light blinked and the air in the space undulated before her. A huge black void opened from the ripple, like a yawning mouth, and instantly a spaceship appeared, hovering for a moment above the grass, whisper quiet. Slowly it settled on the lawn.

With a determination born of a hundred years, Kira stood her ground as she waited for the guards to retrieve her and take her back to a land where she would recognize no one.

As the doors opened, she stood tall. She wouldn't let them see her fear. Wouldn't let them know the horror of the past hundred years. The loneliness. The pain she had endured being torn apart from her loved ones.

A male figured emerged from the ship, gingerly holding the handrails, hunched over and walking tentatively as if each step were painful. People stood guard next to the man, holding onto his arms so he wouldn't fall. When he got to the ground, he raised his rheumy eyes to her.

Beautiful green eyes.

With a gasp, Kira ran to the old man. "Phasha?" she cried, unbelievably. She stared at him, his head bald, his face a mask of wrinkles, and then he smiled. That beautiful smile. It was as if time stood still for her for the moment. Yes, she could still see him in there.

"My note and star," he said, his voice hoarse. "You're as beautiful as I remember you. I promised I'd wait for you. You were all I ever wanted." He pulled her to him and rubbed her head, and she started crying and hugged him back fiercely.

"Come, Kyralee. I've come to take you home."

But Kyralee shook her head and stepped back. "No, Phasha. Not to Xetathana. That's no longer home for us. If we go back, I'll have only a few years left with you. If we stay on Earth, we can be together forever."

Phasha smiled sadly. "No, my angel. It's not fair to you. If I stay here, I'll always be an old man. I'm not what I was."

Kyralee shook her head and smiled. "Oh, but you're so wrong. You're exactly what you were. You came for me, waited for me, kept yourself alive for me, Phasha. You believed." She grasped his hand in both of hers and ran her fingers across his cheek. "Age can never separate a sun and moon from a note and star, my love." With that, she took a step back and took her lyre in her hands. "Listen to me, Phasha. Listen to my music. Listen to what it does on Earth." She began to play a haunting melody, one of Phasha's favorites, her fingers strumming quickly across the strings.

Phasha froze where he stood, listening raptly. Kyralee picked up the pace, her fingers strumming and plucking faster and faster until he could no longer see them moving. They were but a whirl in front of him. She kept playing, watching for the moment Phasha was about to totter and fall down, and then she stopped.

As if waking from a dream, he blinked his eyes, trying to remember where he was. He turned to Kyralee, and flinched in surprise. His eyes widened and Kyralee smiled triumphantly.

It had worked.

Kyralee watched as Phasha stood taller and took a hesitant step, unaided. His gait was stronger, his balance a bit better. He took a deep breath, then another and then turned back to his people. "Return to Xetathana. I will be staying here," he ordered, his voice no longer hoarse.

The guards seemed shaken themselves from the effects of the music upon them, but on their king's command moved away and into the airship. Within seconds they disappeared in the ripple of air and it was silent in the park once again.

Phasha turned to Kyralee and she took his hand. "It may take years for me to safely undo the ravages of time, but it can be done in this world. And then we'll be together, for always."

Phasha smiled sadly. "But what will you do after you've returned me to my youth, Kyralee? Will you never play your instrument again? Can you do that? It's who you are. It's your very essence."

Kyralee smiled. "Love is about sacrifice, Phasha. And it's one I'll gladly make."

And with that, they moved together across the Great Lawn and disappeared into the park, leaving Xetathana far behind.

The Soul Gardener

Ann Swann

The Soul Gardener

The first time I realized I was different, really knew it with my brain rather than just suspecting it in my heart, was Valentine's Day 2011 when I went into the women's restroom at Fiddlesticks Restaurant during a lull in the evening shift.

It had been a long day, and I was just about beat. I'd had to go to school early to make up a Social Studies test I'd missed on Monday due to fever and a sore throat. Felt like I was coming down with something, but after a little rest, I was back to normal.

It wouldn't hurt me to miss a day or two. I'd been skipped ahead a couple of times over the years. Mom said I had an eidetic memory. Guess it's true. If I read it, I remembered it.

And yet, baby genius or not, there I was on St. Valentine's Day, waiting tables just like always. Not that I really cared, but I was supposed to have a date since I was scheduled to be off. So what if it was only with Brett, my best friend since junior high? We were supposed to go see the repeat of *My Bloody Valentine* at the old refurbished Rialto Theater on Shadow Street. But then Carrie Ann called in sick and dear old Mom volunteered me to cover her shift. Strangely enough, she had never done that before without asking me first. In light of what happened later, it turned out to be quite fateful. Anyway, I never had a choice. Mom's the manager at Fiddlesticks.

She says I have to earn my way just like everyone else, and that just because I'm smart doesn't mean I'm smart enough. I couldn't figure that one out for a long time...then I did. It means I need common sense to go along with my book-smarts. And common sense usually comes from a background of experience, not just text book learning. According to Mom, anyhow.

Guess she feels the need to push me so hard because it's always been just the two of us. Never knew my dad. To me, he's just a photo in Mom's dresser drawer. She says I didn't miss much, but if she ever does see him again, he has a heck of a lot of explaining to do.

It was after the dinner rush that I took a break and headed for the women's restroom. In front of the mirror, I ran my hands through my straight brown hair in an attempt to ruffle some extra body into it. It was no use. Finally, I gave up and turned to wash. But I couldn't get any soap to come out of the automated dispenser. I knew it wasn't empty. I could see that the barrel of the thing was at least three quarters full. Besides, my Mom would fire the cleaning crew if they let the soap run out. That's a huge deal with her. And if she even *suspected* one of us on the wait staff came out of the bathroom without washing our hands, wow. I can't even imagine the new vocabulary we would learn.

But I was not having any luck this time. I swiped my hands back and forth underneath the spout and...nothing. I jabbed them under one at a time, both together, then back and forth again.

I'd just decided to open it up and see if it was all gunky or something when Maria Callow came out of a stall, strolled over, stuck her hand under the dispenser, and got a palm full of pink goo.

What the heck? I stuck my hands under it again. Nothing.

Maria smiled at me and then activated the Turbo-dry thus cutting off any chance of conversation.

Okay. This meant war. I stuck my hands under the soaper again. Still nothing. I stuck them under the faucet. Nada. I fiddled with my hair some more so that Maria wouldn't think I was acting too weird, and as soon as she exited, I ran over to the Turbo and tried it. NOTHING WORKED FOR ME! What the heck was going on?

I gave up, pried the cap off the soap dispenser, and scooped out a dab of pink before realizing I had no way of rinsing. *There's that common sense thing Mom's always harping about.* Okay, Rule #342 for the Common Sense file: Don't soap up if you can't rinse off. I was beginning to think technology was out to get me. There weren't even any paper towels to wipe the mess off my hands.

I got a handful of toilet paper, cleaned off the soap as best I could, then went in search of Mom to tell her our bathroom was on the fritz. Just for good measure, I stuck my hands under the Turbo-dry when I walked by, but nothing happened. *Grrr.*

Giving my limp hair one last pat *(Mom would've killed me for that, too. "Hands off the hair, kiddo," she always said. "Folks don't want to floss before they even finish their meal."),* I hazarded one last glance in the humongous mirror, and that's when the world fell in.

My brown hair wasn't brown anymore. It was pale yellow bordering on white. And my eyebrows? They were gone. Completely. I looked like the vanilla version of Whoopi Goldberg. Or a pastel Mona Lisa minus the funky little smile. If I hadn't been surreptitiously watching Maria in the mirror, I probably would've noticed it earlier.

Must have been the lights.

I looked up at the soft-whites above the counter, but they appeared to be in perfect working order.

I glanced at my reflection again. I looked like some messy child's sidewalk art after a rainstorm. The image made my head swim and my stomach churn. Hand to my middle, I rushed back to the dining room right into the center of the St. Valentine's Day celebration. Maria was handing out roses from table to table while the other members of the wait staff were hurrying about, taking care of the customers. Mom was nowhere to be seen. But there were a bunch of other couples waiting in line, ready to let Cupid take the reins. If I ever have a horse, I thought. I'll name him Cupid. And then I fainted.

When I came to a few seconds later, I was staring directly into the crystal-blue eyes of the most gorgeous creature to ever set foot on land.

I squinched my eyelids shut, convinced I was dreaming.

"Alma? Allie...you all right?" That was Mom's voice. I must not be dreaming after all.

"Hey, there..."

Okay, that was so *not* Mom's voice. It was deep and red. My lids popped open. I didn't want them to. I didn't want to look into those gorgeous eyes again when I was lying flat on my back in the middle of a cadre of waiters and customers. *How embarrassing!* But open, they did. And there he was, black hair shining like the proverbial "glass darkly" that I'd read about.

"Mama?" *Oh, please...how did Mom turn into Mama? That's not what was on my tongue when I last checked.* "Mommy?" *Damn! Who was talking? Me?*

"I'm here, baby. Mama's right here..."

I felt a firm *very pleasurable* pressure on my hand. Mom was squeezing my fingers. Then a cool, damp cloth was placed across my forehead. Mom's hands, I could see them in my peripheral. Wait, if those were Mom's hands, who was squeezing my fingers?

The somehow-pleasurable pressure intensified and then another hand was behind my shoulders lifting and pushing me into a sitting position. *Didn't anyone notice anything smeary about my face?* I raised my free hand to my cheeks to see if I had melted. Everything felt normal.

"Now, then," the red voice said. "Let's get you upright and check for damages, shall we?"

Wow. What was he, a doctor or something? I let my hand fall back to my side. Suddenly, I *did* want to look into those peepers. I felt as though looking into those blue eyes was the only thing that mattered anymore. But his head was turned away. And then, somehow, I was up and walking.

Red Voice had helped me to my feet, and with Mom at my elbow, they managed to get me to her office. For a moment I faltered, the industrial carpet felt rough, but when Red Voice leaned down to scoop up my knees so that he could carry me the rest of the way, I said, "Umm, no. I'm okay. I can walk." And I did, with just a bit of a stumble.

Mom kept a mirror inside her office closet (along with a change of clothes and a complete set of make-up identical to the one she kept in the bathroom drawer at home), and I wanted to pop open that door and have a look at my face, but no. Red Voice was intent on depositing me onto the sofa. From a distance, through the open office door, I could hear the sounds of the restaurant getting back to normal. Maria was telling the customers I had suffered an attack of low blood sugar and I would be fine after a bit.

I felt like such an idiot. But at the same time, all my senses seemed heightened. And my feet were bare. Where were my shoes? I glanced down at my feet, and that's when things got really weird.

Mom was scurrying about, getting me cookies and juice as if I'd just donated blood, when Red Voice leaned over and whispered, "You can stop thinking of me as Red Voice, and your shoes are still in the dining room where you fainted."

I don't know which opened wider, my eyes or my mouth. "You read minds?"

He threw his head back and laughed heartily. "Of course not. You've been muttering *red voice* for the last minute or two."

I clapped my hands over my mouth. *Oooh. Bad idea.* Sudden movements were apparently verboten. My stomach rose up in revolt, but I refused to be attacked by technology and my own body all in the space of half an hour so I sat up gingerly, and looked him straight in the eye. "Do I know you?" *Oh, my last word, those green eyes were killing me!*

He hesitated a fraction of a second longer than he should have. "No. We haven't met."

I knew he wasn't telling me the whole truth. It might not be a lie, but still...I sensed something not right.

His face was ruddy. *Maybe that's why I'd thought his voice sounded red. At that second, anything seemed possible.* And the hue of his skin was a startling contrast to those brilliant green eyes. And the hair. Wow. That thick blond hair. It was like a lion's mane. I wanted to touch it, run my fingers through it, see if it was coarse or fine or—

I had to say something, quickly. Or I was going to make a bigger fool of myself than I'd already done.

"I'm Allie," I said. As if he hadn't heard Mom calling my name a few moments earlier.

"No," he replied. "You're Alma. It means soul. But you knew that already."

"What? Oh, sure." I hoped my attempt at deception wasn't as transparent as it felt. I should have known that, shouldn't I? I mean, it was my own name, after all.

"Alma?"

I looked at him. Actually, now that I had my wits about me again, I couldn't stop looking at him. "Yes?" Why did I ever think his voice was red? It was black silk, pure and simple. And those deep brown eyes…wait a minute! *Brown?*

"Alma, what?" he asked. "What is the rest of your name?" Something in the timbre of his voice stilled me. I was about to ask him about his eyes, his hair, and the changing shade of his now alabaster skin. But even the air had stilled. The dining room sounds were nonexistent. And my mom, where had she disappeared to all of a sudden?

"Umm," my voice worked, but it didn't seem to be connected to my brain. "My name? Kai. Alma Kai Gardner." There. That wasn't so bad. I could speak when spoken to after all. Eventually I might even master complete sentences again.

His face was pensive. "Alma means soul," he said. "Kai means key." He waited patiently, to make sure I was following. "And Gardner is a term meaning exactly what it sounds like, a gardener." His blue-gray eyes darkened. "Alma Kai Gardner.

Key to the garden of souls…is that you Alma Kai?" His voice had grown deeper, even more seductive than before. Now it was dark, cocoa brown.

"Huh?" I gazed at him in wonderment. *Where was that darned intelligence when I needed it? What was he talking about? Where had he even come from? Oh yeah, I fainted. Must still be out cold.*

An idea occurred to me. I must've suffered some sort of brain episode, a seizure or maybe something as simple as a migraine. I'd read that some people saw auras and flashing lights just before the onset of a migraine. Some even hallucinated. Yes! That must be it. That must be what was happening to me.

Now, I was *determined* to look at the mirror on the inside of that closet door. But I didn't want Mr. Wonderful to wonder what I was doing. And I didn't want to look at him again, in case he wasn't really there. *Actually, I wanted nothing more than to sit and look at him, but what if I couldn't quit?* No, right now, I'd better just look at me. I glanced down at my hands and arms. Everything appeared to be all right except for the fact that my bare feet were itching like crazy. A sudden crazy thought lit up my brain: *I shed my shoes. Now am I going to shed my itchy skin?*

"You're changing," he said.

I ran my palms up and down my suddenly itchy arms recalling how none of the automatic dispensers would work for me in the restroom. And that image in the mirror… I didn't want to think about that again. "Changing?" I asked. "What do you mean?"

"Come," he offered his hand.

"Where we going?" I grasped his fingers and stood slowly. The feel of his flesh on mine was as pleasurable and intoxicating as before. The longer I was near him, the more intoxicating it became. *What was happening to me?*

He strode directly to Mom's closet and opened the door. "Have a look," he said. "And then I'll tell you why nothing seems to work right anymore."

Suddenly, I was terrified. I did not want to see what might be peering out at me from that square of shiny acrylic.

"No," I said softly. "No, don't make me look." *A moment earlier I'd been desperate to see.* "Please, just tell me what's going on."

I looked into his face instead of into the mirror. His eyes were as black as onyx, the brows thick and straight, and his hair was the ripest shade of auburn. *Had his nose lengthened and thickened a bit when I'd looked away? Sort of like a muzzle? No, just another weird trick of the light or something. He still looked every bit as gorgeous as before.*

"You're beginning to see, aren't you?" he asked. "You're beginning to see me as I really am. No one else in the world can look at me the way you do. Or see me as I am." His voice was deep red again, to match the color of his hair.

"I don't know what I see. You seem to change back and forth, your eyes, your hair, your skin—"

He smiled and the teeth behind the lips were feral, magnificent. "My name is Ambrose Wolfhardt," he said. "I know you studied Greek and Latin."

I scanned my memory. Yes. "Ambrose is Greek. It means immortal. But Wolfhardt isn't Greek or Latin. It's Germanic. It means having the heart of a wolf." My breath escaped my chest in a low hushing sound. "Germany. The Black Forest. Wolves. Legends. *Werewolves!*" I looked at him again. His eyes were yellow, his hair a smooth and lovely shade of winter ash. *"Now, I see."*

He closed his eyes. "No. Not *werewolf.* Not anymore. I've changed, too. Now, I am simply a shape-shifter." There was steel beneath his words. Or perhaps it was just the ring of truth.

I turned to the mirror, eyes closed. He said he had changed, *too*. What did that mean? Did he know something I didn't? What did he see when he looked at me?

I steadied my resolve and opened my eyes. My tanned, angular face was now round, peach colored, and soft as the love in a mother's eye. My brown hair was bright. Brighter than the frothy whitecap on a roiling ocean wave. And my wings, my glorious, inexplicable wings, were the same pearl gray as the breast of a mourning dove. They perfectly matched my once-blue eyes.

I inhaled shakily. But I was not afraid. I had always known I was different. I caressed my wings with trembling fingers. "Where did they come from? Am I a shape-shifter, too?"

Gently, he turned me from the mirror to face him. The tips of my wings brushed the ceiling when they opened of their own accord. "You're a seraph, an angel of the highest order. The keeper of the key to the garden of souls." Then he whispered. "And I have lost my soul."

The anguish in his quicksilver voice was heart wrenching. I wanted to help him. It occurred to me there was nothing I wouldn't do for this creature. But if I were an angel…should I really feel such a powerful *attraction*? There must be some mistake. I was just a girl. *With wings and sea foam hair?*

"The garden of souls?" I felt a breeze fan my face as my wings closed. Everything was so strange. *Now I know how the butterfly feels when it escapes the cocoon.* I practiced fluttering a few times. All of Mom's papers flew off her desk and onto the floor. "I don't know anything about a key, or the garden, or anyone's soul," I said. "But now I guess I know why technology no longer works for me." I laughed softly. "Am I human at all?"

He ignored my question. Instead he said, "Look." He pointed down the hall toward the dining room. It was as if we were standing at the end of a lengthy tunnel. Everything was far away, distorted, fuzzy. "We must leave," he said. "Are you ready?"

I squeezed his fingers. "I think so. But my mom. What about my mom?"

"Trust me," he replied. "Just…trust."

And so I did. I'd finally accepted that this was no hallucination. Or if it was, I didn't want it to end. *Angel? Of course I'd heard of angels. The term was bandied about so often and so lightly, that I'd never considered it might have a basis rooted in fact. But soul keeper? Me?*

"I have to show you how I lost my soul," he said. "It isn't pretty. In fact, it's pretty horrific." His eyes were black again, his hair a sleek and feathered sable. He held both my hands, and to my astonishment, huge ragged wings sprouted from his back. They dwarfed my pearl-gray ones. He was an eagle, at least he had the wings of an eagle, but the rest of him remained, wholly, a man.

"Before we go to the garden," he continued. "I want you to understand why I was the way I was. And why I am the way I am now." His voice had grown rougher, as though the words were actually painful. "We'll go to ancient Greece first. Start at the beginning."

"But it no longer exists," I said. "How can we...?" Then I realized what I was saying. I had just morphed, he had just morphed, what was a little time travel on top of all that?

"We can," he insisted. "Together, we can go anywhere. Simply open your wings. And your heart." He touched me gently, just beneath my chin.

I closed my eyes and opened my wings. The ceiling rippled and disappeared. He dropped my left hand, gripped my right one even tighter and we were flying, floating above the restaurant, above the town, above the clouds, and as we rose, the world slipped away below us, and around us, and possibly, through us.

In moments we were standing on top of Mount Olympus, looking down on a new landscape, a stone-floored great-room in an ancient Greek palace. "What *is* that?" I cried. The scene below me was one of absolute chaotic fear. Men in blood-spattered white tunics were running this way and that. On a tremendous stone table that could have doubled as an altar, overturned goblets and dishes were strewn about, filthy with scraps of meat and ripe fruits. And then I saw it. The bloody remains of a child lay in the midst of the huge table.

"Oh my God!" My hand covered my mouth, but I couldn't look away. "Is this why you lost your soul?" I looked at my companion in horror. "Did you do this?"

He was shaking his shaggy head back and forth. I could see that the scene was even harder for him to watch than it was for me. "This was my home." The words almost choked him. "My father, Lyacon, King of Arcadia, doubted Zeus's divinity. He tried to trick the god into eating the flesh of my brother as a test."

I looked back at the slab table. "That boy was your brother?"

He ground out the words. "My father had many sons. He thought nothing of using us for his own gain. He made my brother appear as a succulent lamb on the spit."

It suddenly dawned on me. I'd read this myth. "But Zeus wasn't fooled," I said. "He turned King Lyacon into a man-wolf—"

"And in his rage, my father turned on the rest of his sons, attacking us and forcing his foul blackness into our bloodline." At last, he hung his magnificent head. His wings drooped from his shoulder blades. The blue sky began to dissolve into darkness, but not before I saw the werewolf-king attempting to devour another one of his own children on the stone floor below. "That one was me," he said quietly. "I survived. But for eons, I wished I hadn't."

Then he sat me down beneath a jagged overhang of rock, and regaled me with terrible tales of the things he'd done and the people he'd killed in order to survive during the many lifetimes he'd already lived. "But it wasn't until Roanoke that I lost my soul."

"Virginia?"

He softly turned my head to the side and showed me another ethereal video from the past.

I could see a fleet of seven smallish ships with tall masts. As we watched, supplies were loaded and men, women, and children milled about, waiting to board. One of the ships was named *The Lion*. It was the only one I could read from this distance.

Ambrose motioned toward a couple of men standing apart from the others. "Do you see the one in the dark umber cloak?"

I looked, nodded.

"Ambrose Wolfhardt, in human form, bound for The New World. I was ready for a new start. Europe had waged war on me and my remaining brothers." His voice was sad. "The ones who escaped Zeus's lightning bolts. My father did not, thank the gods."

Still watching the activity on the dock, I spied a tall man, nattily dressed, an accordion collar making him stand out like a prince among paupers. He was busy giving orders and signing papers. "Sir Walter Raleigh," I guessed, having seen his famous countenance in history books.

"Yes. Our benefactor. We were en route to Virginia, but the Captain, a pirate named Simon Fernandes, put the lot of us off at a deserted island-settlement called Roanoke."

"Of course, I know that story, too."

A shadow fell over his face. My sympathy was aroused again, and once more, he bade me watch his memories. This time it was a Native American settlement barely visible through the trees. "My new start," he said simply.

"Okay," I said. "I'm smart, I'm not psychic…or am I?" I looked at him to see if he had any sense of humor at all.

He smiled wryly. "I was starved by the time Fernandes deserted us at Roanoke. I'd fed sparingly on the journey, and after a few weeks passed, I simply lost control. I really had intended to make a new start. Live on animals, like the animal I was. But I hadn't counted on such easy prey tossed right into my lap." His face was bathed in shadow.

Understanding dawned on me like a light in a dark room. "*You* were the cause of the disappearance of the colonists of Roanoke?"

"I didn't catch them all…a few escaped. But I was in a blood frenzy. On top of my hunger, the moon was full and the colonists were weak from travelling…"

"Why didn't you—?" He stilled my question with a look that said he had but one breath with which to finish the tale.

"A shaman from the Croatan tribe happened upon me during my feast." His hair turned black as I watched. His eyes melted back to deep brown. But his wings stayed the same raggedy mix of brown, white and gray shades.

"What happened?" I asked.

Ambrose gripped my fingers. "He lured me to a cave, and there he captured me in a web of incantations that drove the curse from my body. But it was too late for my soul. The shaman saw it leave. He said it flew up to the garden to await my return. He said a soul could not partake of the amount of evil that I had visited upon the Earth—but since it had not been my choice, rather a curse bestowed upon me by my father—I might be allowed another chance at goodness. At life. If I could locate the keeper of the key."

"Still not psychic," I said, my confusion evident on my face.

"He was able to free me from the curse of lycanthropy, but in its place, I became what you see now, a shape-shifter." Then he pointed to a spot in the near distance. "Do you see the garden?"

I let my gaze follow his finger. I thought I could see something shimmering in the air. It appeared to be a rainbow trapped in the cup of the mountaintop.

"That's where my soul should be." He grazed my cheek with his forefinger as he spoke.

I felt as if the sharp black talon sprouting from its tip should repulse me, but I found that it bothered me not at all. I pulled it to my lips and kissed it tenderly.

His eyes closed and his body grew very still. "Not while I am in this form," he murmured. "Not while I am soulless." He curled his claws into his palm and pulled me to him roughly.

For a moment I was frightened, but not afraid. I didn't understand it myself. But I knew he would not hurt me. I placed both my palms against his chest and let the pulse of his heart play into my hands. "Tell me," I said. "What happens now?"

"I need my soul," he replied. "I'm no longer evil, but I'm also no longer whole. In fact, I think I'm running out of time." He flapped his wings and smiled sadly. "I went from killer werewolf to half-formed eagle. I have no control over my body. It changes at will."

"Then we must be off." I glanced down at the pastel shimmers that signified the garden, and suddenly, we were there.

Wow! I think I'm going to like this flying business!

I gazed around at the wide, walled, meadow. Every flower in existence bloomed in wild profusion along the walls and pathways. It was the most fantastic place I'd ever imagined. At one end was an immense gate covered over with roses, at the other end, an open-air pavilion as green and shady as any forest glen on Earth.

Ambrose walked along the curving path, his wings appearing and disappearing as I watched. In moments, the thick, tawny mane of a lion enshrouded his face and neck. Yet he barely seemed to notice. "Alma Kai, keeper of the Garden, where is my soul, pray tell?"

I hurried to catch up with him. My wings did not disappear, instead, they tilted and eddied and balanced themselves on my back in such a fashion that within moments I was right beside him. "Ambrose…wait. I don't know where the *key* is hidden, much less your *soul*."

He stopped for a moment, head cocked, and I thought he was about to tell me how to find the key, but then he tackled me and threw me to the ground. My wings crumpled beneath me and I had a moment to think, *it was all a ruse! He hasn't changed at all. He wants the head of a Seraphim as a trophy on his den wall.*

I struggled to escape his immense weight pinning me to the ground, and that's when I heard the high-pitched song of a howling wolf.

Craning my head around, I peeked over his thick mane and became aware of another sound…a deep bass growl rumbling up from the belly of my captor. In moments it burst from his throat as a terrific roar. I covered my ears and closed my eyes expecting to be devoured. And then the weight left me. I cringed, certain I was about to be yanked up and ripped limb from limb.

But I was wrong. The growling roar intensified as it met and blended with the howls from outside the wall. I opened my eyes just in time to see Ambrose, the winged lion, flash up to the open sky and crash headlong into a huge, slavering werewolf that had leapt to the top of the stonewall.

Snout full of daggers, amber eyes glittering, his snorting breath was as foul as death, even from a distance. He was at least as big as my lion, maybe even bigger.

"Ambrose!" I screamed.

He didn't respond. His human form was completely gone. He had turned into a gryphon, that mythological beast with the head and wings of an eagle, body of a lion, and the tail of a deadly serpent.

I watched as the great wolf loomed up on hind legs and attempted to rake his saber-like teeth across Ambrose's throat.

In response, Ambrose curled his claws into the soft underbelly of the wolf. His serpent's tail struck the animal's hindquarters repeatedly, spitting poison from two-inch fangs as its head drove in again and again. When the wolf attempted to swat the snake with its razor-claws, Ambrose ripped his own feline claws upward, disemboweling the lycanthrope handily.

"Watch out!" I screamed again.

Ambrose spun, slinging his snake-tail like a whip around the throat of the second wolf, which had just bounded onto the wall behind him. Yanking back with a mighty roar, he popped the wolf's head clean off its shoulders. I thought it would fall directly into the garden of souls beside me, dead. But as I watched, the bloody mass tumbled end over end and tried to restore itself even though the torso fell a dozen feet from the severed head. I had to look away as the horrid snout continued to snap and howl soundlessly. *What could I do to help?* Two more wolves had jumped onto the wide wall and were advancing on my gryphon from either side.

Suddenly, an idea occurred to me. If the werewolves were here to prevent him from regaining his soul, then perhaps if I could find and restore it *while he was in battle* it would make him that much stronger! It was all I could think of. *But where to find a gryphon's soul?* Where would the soul of an immortal beast choose to rest? *Immortal! That was the key.* I'd read somewhere that frangipani was the flower of the Immortals. *That had to be it.*

As the two new werewolves closed in on Ambrose, I flew through the garden in search of the fragrant flower. Upon its petals, I was certain I would find the soul of my shape-shifter. But just as I caught scent of the fantastic fragrance, a tremendous thud resounded from the top of the high wall. I glanced back just in time to see Ambrose swooping back down upon the two wolves who had collided when he flew up out of their reach. Curved black claws fully extended, Ambrose landed upon the pair of them slashing and scratching, his eagle's beak as sharp and deadly as one of his lion's claws.

For an instant, I hovered in place, mesmerized by the horror. Then from out of nowhere, another wolf hurtled into the fray and the four of them crashed to the ground on the opposite side of the wall. The last thing I saw was a glimpse of a great, ragged wing in the mouth of an ancient wolf. *Three on one. My heart began to gallop with dread. I had to find his soul. Quickly!*

Seeing no frangipani, but certain I could smell their sweet scent, I cruised up and down the pathways, searching. Flowers of all kinds glimmered with souls like drops of colorful dew upon their petals. But no frangipani! I was certain I would recognize it if I saw it, I recalled pictures of the five-petal blooms from encyclopedias I had read through the years. Wait! What was I thinking? It wasn't a flower *per se*, it was a flowering tree or at the very least, a flowering bush.

Now I knew where to look.

A sickening cry of rage split the air. My winged lion raked his claws across the wet black nose of the largest wolf. The two of them had regained the top of the wall as I rushed back across the garden to the lovely orchards we'd flown over only moments earlier.

Yet, even as the large wolf retreated, howling with pain, another one dove in beneath Ambrose in an attempt to rip at his underbelly with those dagger-like teeth. This one was smaller, faster, and even fiercer than the others.

Screeching, Ambrose swiped at the wolf and pushed off on the larger creature's back with his strong hind paws and the help of those immense wings. The smaller wolf tumbled over and over toward the ground, its center of balance momentarily demolished.

As I flew, I kept one eye on the smaller wolf. He wasn't retreating, only recuperating, shaking his ghastly head, the sharp points of his fangs sparkling in the sun as though tipped with steel.

I saw the serpent tail of the gryphon sink its fangs into the larger wolf, but then—

"Ambrose!" I cried. It was too late. The smaller wolf bounced back like a spring and slid under my gryphon's belly, slashing him chest to groin with those razor-sharp teeth.

With a terrible shriek, Ambrose turned on the smaller wolf and sliced the heart out of it with barely a pause. The two of them fell from the wall and lay just inside the garden, blood seeping into the hallowed soil. The larger wolf had fallen to the opposite side of the wall, out of sight. I had to hurry...the life of an immortal might be hard to take, but obviously it was possible if the injury was imposed by another immortal. And he'd said he was running out of time even before the battle.

And that's when I saw salvation in the corner of the orchard. A profusion of frangipani trees and bushes loaded with gorgeous yellow, white, and pink blossoms growing in such thick abandon that their fantastic scent wafted across the entire garden.

I rushed headlong toward the orchard, gazing at the abundance of flowers in dismay. Each petal held a beautiful soul...how would I ever determine which one belonged to my love?

Then I saw it, a brilliant purple orb of light shining forth from the depths of an ancient, twisted frangipani tree covered with creamy white blossoms. Purple was for royalty, I thought. As royal as a lion, or the son of a Greek king. I rushed to capture the sparkling sphere of light but there was no need, it fairly leapt into my hand...I could only hope it wasn't too late.

Just as the lighter-than-air soul graced my palm, I heard a second horrific cry of pain as the larger wolf reappeared, landing on Ambrose from the top of the wall.

"No!" I rushed forward, wings as blurry as a hummingbird headed into a hurricane. Without hesitation, I flew straight to my love, the soul vibrating in my grasp. Opening my fist, the shimmering orb flew into the heaving chest, the ugly gash closing behind it as the purple light grew dimmer and dimmer until the entire wound was no more.

The large werewolf's fiery eyes locked onto mine. But I had no worry now. Ambrose had his soul. With a war cry ferocious enough to split open the world, he leapt to his feet—all four of them—and slung the last demon off his back as though the huge lycanthrope was nothing more than a bothersome gnat.

The wolf immediately began to change into human form in an attempt to escape the gryphon's leonine claws. But it was only half-shifted when Ambrose decapitated it just like the other one. He gathered the human head and all the wolfen body parts and flew them to the top of Mount Olympus where he flung them off the other side.

When he landed beside me again, I sensed a difference. "Will they come back?"

He enclosed me inside those powerful wings. "They're gone," he said. "Their only reason for still existing was to prevent me from finding you and regaining my soul."

I watched as his shape began to change even as he held me. In moments, the gore-streaked mane was gone, replaced by the shiny, black hair I remembered seeing when I woke up on the floor of the restaurant a mini-lifetime ago. The wide shoulders and crystal-blue eyes had also returned. All of him was human again except for the raggedy wings. They seemed to be a permanent fixture.

"Does this mean you get to stay with me now?" I looked into his eyes and they did not change color, not even once.

"I think it does," he nodded. "I'm new at this, too, you know. But since I've got nothing better to do…"

I slugged him on the arm, but he pulled me back to his chest and held me tightly as the sun raced behind a cloud and a terrific storm opened up the heavens.

We took shelter in the depths of a wisteria-covered gazebo. Within moments, the entire scene had been washed clean and the garden was fresh and fragrant once more.

As the rain stopped, and the sun peeked out of hiding, I glanced around, taking stock of my souls. They were everywhere, on every flower petal, a rainbow of color sparkling and winking in the light of the sun. "I never did find that key," I said, remembering.

Ambrose laughed gently. "It was you," he said. "You *are* the key."

I snuggled deeper into his embrace, and tilted my face up for his kiss.

An eternity later, we broke apart. "Come with me," he said, breath light against my lips. "There is one more thing you have to see..."

And then we were hovering over the restaurant again. "There's my mom," I said, tears springing to my eyes. "She looks so sad."

"Watch," Ambrose said. "Wait."

A man strode into the restaurant holding a bouquet of flowers. Even from my atmosphere of invisibility, I could smell the scent of those flowers. "That's my father!"

Ambrose nodded. "He will make your mother happy now."

"But she'll miss me." I knew she wouldn't just forget about me.

"No, she won't forget you," he said, reading my mind again. "But it will be as if you never were."

He must have seen the stricken look in my eyes, for he rushed to explain.

"You and your father couldn't co-exist on the same plane of reality. He passed the gardener's genes to you. Only now could he return."

Finally, I understood, but still. "My mom..."

Ambrose's voice was kind. "Sometimes she will get a feeling of déjà vu, and she may grow melancholy for no good reason, but the feeling will pass. You will send her the scent of forget-me-nots and all will be right again. And we will be together in the garden of souls where all my sins will be rewritten because you love me."

I still wasn't positive that everything he was saying was true, or would be true, but as we floated back toward my garden in the cup of Mount Olympus, I watched my mother rush across the floor to my long-lost father. Once again we were enveloped in the heady aroma of a dozen different flowers as the Valentine's Day bouquet was crushed between them, in their embrace.

"Hey," I caressed my love's beautiful face. "There's still something I don't understand."

He took my hands and held them against his chest. His face was open, trustworthy.

"How'd you find me, after all this time? Right on the very day I began to change..."

He looked into my eyes and I felt as if I could see all the way to his soul. I knew he was about to impart some deep kernel of wisdom he'd gleaned over the centuries, something the shaman had taught him, perhaps. Something no other human being on Earth could possibly know. He was about to tell me what miracle had led him here, to me, after all this time.

"Well?"

Joyful laughter prevented him from speaking. He laughed so long and so robustly that I began to get annoyed.

"What's so funny?" I demanded, my once-human-teenage-girl-attitude coming out. "Don't make me sorry I restored your soul you...you animal!" I pulled my hands free of his grasp and opened my wings, about to see how fast they could fly.

"No," he said, tears streaming. "Don't be mad. It's just that, it's so simple."

I stood silently, tapping my bare foot, ineffectually, on a puffy pile of cumulus clouds. "Okay, and why is it so funny?"

He inhaled mightily, barked a few more uncontrollable guffaws, and then straightened his shaking shoulders. "It was that," he said, pointing down at the restaurant.

"The Valentine's Day special?" My common sense was not helping with this at all. And I definitely was not psychic. In fact, I may as well have been a moron.

"Not the special," he said. "Not exactly." He was being patient, but his shoulders were still quaking with silent laughter. "That," he pointed toward the advertisement once more.

"Cupid?" My eyes had finally registered the only other thing on the window, a big shiny red-foil Cupid. "You mean to tell me he's real?" The absurdity of my question hit me as soon as the words left my now-angelic lips.

"Oh, he's real," my immortal assured me. "And it appears he works in very mysterious ways."

The Scratcher

Denise Vitola

The Scratcher

There is a story from District 19 that tells of a man who once ate a whole car. He carved it into tiny pieces and savored the metal, the torn leather, the oily engine, and the rusty bits. He said he was hungry enough that he enjoyed every morsel, likening it to a grass-fed cow with each bite tasting of filet mignon.

I was that hungry. The last time my lips touched food was two days ago, and then it was only a half-rotten tater I stole from a street vendor. But there were no cars here with which to make a meal. This was Pompeii, and it was August 23rd, AD 79.

Darting through the crowded Marcellum, I shouldered Roman women as they bartered with merchants for their daily bread and fish. Kids taunted me and men shouted when I rushed through the backs of their stalls, knocking over bins of produce in my attempt to keep ahead of the trouble. Most stopped to stare at me because here was a young woman with short blonde hair, carrying a bulging leather sack and wearing cotton churidar pants and a kurta top—men's clothing that I had picked up in India. I'm sure there was something illegal about it, but that was the least of my worries.

A shout rose behind me. Some Latin invective or a helpful word to my pursuers. To these fine citizens of the Roman Empire, I was being chased by *cohortes urbanae,* the police of the time. Only these weren't fine soldiers doing their duty for the emperor. These were Michael's men—hand selected Humans who thought the Arch Commander was the war god, Mars. Idiots.

I dashed by a butcher wielding a cleaver over a hunk of meat and swung down a narrow alley between the stone buildings, running past a parade of filthy prostitutes. I could hear the clink of armor when the unit turned the corner after me. Just when I thought I could feel their hot, garlicky breath on my neck, someone reached out from a darkened alcove and yanked me into the shadows.

It was a big guy with long, dark hair and a close-cropped beard. He angled his body in front of mine, shielding me from the oncoming soldiers. They clanked by, disappearing toward the public baths, several whores treading after them. I didn't move until I heard the last stomping footfall fade away.

My savior stepped back into the light. He studied me before smiling, his light blue eyes sparkling. "You would be Esa, I presume?"

I nodded. "Thomas?"

"That's me." He paused to glance along the length of the alley. "Come on."

We scooted along close to the buildings until we emerged onto an eerie neighborhood in the middle of the main city. The buildings were ramshackle, their facades filthy with red clay and the dark dust from peat fires. Greasy, ragged curtains billowed from the black holes of windows and the doors to the houses, painted with swirly symbols meant to keep away the evil eye, were further decorated with crude graffiti. Open sewers swelled with trash. I tried to take small breaths because the smell of urine and poop was enough to curl my nose hairs. We passed a scuffed up bronze statue of the goddess Venus, pock-marked by the weather. It guarded the entrance to a brothel where there were no signs of customers—or of life. This avenue was unnaturally silent and as if to proclaim it a place of the dead, I saw no people, but everywhere I looked I could see the ephemeral presence of ghosts. I noticed a placard nailed to the side of a crumbling garden wall. *Via de' Umbra*—Shadow Street.

Thomas led me into the last house on the left, slamming and locking the heavy wooden door behind us. Surprisingly, I found myself in a clean home, sparsely decorated with a table, chair, and a narrow bed. There was a brick oven in the far corner, already hot, the acrid scent of decaying vegetable matter not all that discomfiting after the vile nuances of the outside air. I glanced into the small opening to see an iron pot settled in the hot peat ashes. Food. I nearly fainted at the thought. Thomas didn't speak, but I'm sure he noticed my drooling. He smiled, pointing to the chair before moving to dish up a bowl of dinner. It was some kind of stew, probably cow ears and spleens, but it had the scent of ambrosia. I dropped my sack and gratefully dove into the meal. He pulled up a stool while I shoveled the grisly, slimy concoction into my pie hole.

You may think that I'm just your average person moving about her day, but the truth is a lot stranger and an eye-opener. I'm a Nephalim, the daughter of a Human mother and an Angelic-Annunaki male. Down through the centuries, the stories were woven about the Watchers, those Angels who fell to Earth, banished from Heaven.

The truth is, the Annunaki were space travelers who came here in vast ships, searching for gold to create their O'rmis, the white powder they needed for inter-dimensional travel. They discovered this tiny world on a far reef in a lonely galaxy. When they got here, they created a slave race by selectively adding their supernormal genes with the lower mammalian life forms. They added just enough goo to the pot that Humans would obey, but not enough to understand free will. The Watchers changed all that by falling in love with their own creations and tried to elevate the species through a bold blending of alien DNA. Every Human ever born carries the genetic markers granted to them by the Annunaki and their large, capable brains are a gift of Lumiel and his brethren.

Thomas silently studied me as I grunted and groaned over the food. He was as beautiful as a full blood Angelic-Annunaki could be. There were three castes, each hailing from a different planet but forged as the same species—Pearls, those who had wings of white feathers, the Slates, creatures bearing gray feathered wings, and the Leathers, individuals who over the course of history were erroneously named demons. I understood that Thomas was a Slate. He, like his fellows, had been stripped of much of their power, but they still had the ability to atomically phase their wings, making them invisible to the naked eye until they chose to use them.

"Thank you for coming," he murmured.

I talked around a piece of unknown flesh. "Not a problem. If we pull this off, the payout for me will be much appreciated."

He nodded. "How long have you been hiding in the corridors of the past?"

Thomas's words made being on the lam sound romantic. "Zachary spirited me away about five Earth cycles ago. I've been marching around the Far East for a while, honing my craft."

"How were things in the 21st century? I haven't been up-time for a while."

I blew a steam of air through my nostrils. The truth was Thomas couldn't move up-time because of a nasty run in with Gabriel. That's why I was here. "The 21st century is crapped. Disease, poverty and war. Michael keeps things bloody."

Thomas grunted. "Him and his flaming sword of justice. I hope he breaks the damned thing one day. In fact, if I ever get the chance, I'll do it."

I stopped spooning spleen to study this gorgeous creature. It is unusual for me to have an instant rapport with an Angelic, but he was different. He exuded fierceness, tempered with an odd sort of gentleness. "You really care about Humans, don't you?"

"I was the Angel who wrote down the Word, Esa," he said. "And I was the one who taught Humanity to read and write."

"You were one of the Progenitors?" I asked, stunned.

"I was." He paused, then said, "I am. But being trapped, I can't do much to help the Children as I once did. Illiteracy retakes its place within a generation."

That was big stuff. The Progenitors directed the Watchers to secretly give the people a chance to evolve by teaching them sacred knowledge. "Michael and his cronies must hate you."

He shrugged. "Let's just say I'm on their top-ten list of undesirables. It's complicated, though."

"You're the one who has a chance for redemption. I've heard stories."

"Maybe. I've thrown in with Lumiel in his efforts to get the O'rmis into the population. If Michael finds out, I'm toast."

O'rmis was a miracle element. Not only did it enable the Angelic-Annunaki to trip the light fantastic, but when it was imbibed by the lower breeds, it turned on locked genes, enabling the species to make remarkable advances in their evolution. Michael was in charge of keeping it away from Nephalim and Humans alike, because it was impossible to control a world of brilliant, self-actualizing individuals. The story was the Elohim had tasked him to keep Earthlings as dumb as cinderblocks. It had worked until the day he had pissed off Lumiel.

Thomas stood up, moving to a crooked wooden shelf above the bed. He pulled down a small Roman glass bottle and filled it with water from a nearby bucket. He then dug out a rush mat and spread it on the floor. "I don't mean to hurry you, Esa, but we have to get started. Tomorrow is D-Day around here."

Oh, that was right. "Sorry I'm late. I literally took a slow boat from China." I finished eating and collected my rucksack. Sitting on the floor, I set up my equipment by the mat. Thomas removed his simple, brown robe, and stood bare-chested before me. I laughed when I saw he had on a pair of boxer shorts. They had red hearts on them.

He grinned, but said nothing, instead stretching out on the mat, and presenting his back to me. He was a taut-muscled hunk. It took my breath away.

"How many have you done of these?" he asked quietly.

"About a hundred."

"Ever had a failure?"

"Once. I was rushed."

"Like now?"

I bit my lip. "It will be fine. I work fast. I only hope you can keep up with the pain."

"Eh. Pain. It's nothing, sweet Esa. There are so many ways to suffer. This will only be a minor inconvenience. Don't worry."

So, I came to the reason I was here in the first place.

I'm a scratcher for the Angels—that is a tattoo artist—but not an inked-up babe who works in a tattoo parlor. To a Human, what I did would look like magic. It wasn't. It was physics and an innate genetic ability to jigger the first law of thermodynamics.

Since electricity was unknown in the ancient world, I had left behind my tattoo machine and taught myself the art of hand poking. I had spirited several packs of stainless steel sewing needles with me when Zachary had saved me from Michael's crowd. While I hid out in the boreal forests of Siberia, I carved a lovely wooden handle, splitting the end to fit a needle into it. I then wrapped silk thread around and around the base. This was my tattoo tool.

I opened the box of India ink, a powdered concoction of hide glue, carbon black, lampblack, bone black pigment, and most importantly, O'rmis. Placing a spoonful in a small piece of crockery, I dribbled in some of the water and stirred the ink until it turned to liquid. I stabbed the needle into the mixture, letting it saturate the silken thread. The ink would flow down from the silk onto the needle and into Thomas's skin.

"Ready?" I asked.

He grinned. "Get to poking, my new friend."

I did as he asked. The first invasion of my needle brought the drops of blood to the surface. I carefully laid in the ink, wiping away the red stain of his life force. Thomas sighed, not from the pain, but instead from the O'rmis entering his system. O'rmis is the miracle substance, the holy of holies in the Angelic-Annunaki universe.

Hours passed. I worked diligently, scratching out the design onto his back. I poked in the outline of wings, eyes, a beak, and the swirling tail. Day turned into night and I lit several candles to work by, filling in with the intricacy of dot after dot, soft feathers over the entire tattoo. Thomas never said a word, never moaned or jumped when the needle bit deeply into his spine. He was overcome by the presence of O'rmis.

I was affected by the substance, too. It leached into my skin through my fingertips, reopening my inner receptors, what the Roman oracles of the time would call the Third Eye. The O'rmis revealed to me the depth and breadth of the magnificent creature that I touched.

There were images. Some bright, some shadowed. I saw a parade of people whom he cared for and had helped—Humans who wrote words that changed the course of history—such as Homer and his *Iliad*, Dante and his *Divine Comedy*, Christine de Pasan and her *Song of Joan of Arc*. Thomas had been a muse to writers like Charles Dickens, Virginia Woolf, and even Raymond Chandler. He wasn't concerned with whether the person was famous or not. He helped anyone who put a call out to the ethers.

Knowing these things, I slowly became enamored with this Angelic-Annunaki who surrendered his life in a cause to uplift the Human condition.

It was about noon the next day when I laid down the final design segment of the tattoo—a small pile of ash at the base of his spine. I was out of ink and out of O'rmis.

Thomas opened his eyes to stare at me. His pupils were huge and his blue irises were gone. He sat up slowly, twisting his back slightly to relieve the tightness from the ink and the hours of lying on the mat. Taking my stained fingers in his, he caressed my hands. "Thank you," he whispered.

That's when I knew I loved him unconditionally. Call it a crush, simple infatuation, or some whacked out notion of Nephalim romance, but at some point during the tattoo, I'd melded with him. We'd touched spirit to spirit. He'd clubbed me over the head like a beautiful caveman simply by being who he was. At that moment, I understood why Humans said that they felt an overwhelming desire and an unexplainable feeling of love when they encountered an Angel.

Thomas knew it, too. He leaned in toward me and kissed me passionately on the lips. It nearly undid my composure, but I managed to call on my sensible side, telling myself, it was nothing more than a simple thank you. He stood up while I repacked my duffle bag. "We have to hurry," he said. "We only have an hour left."

I finished up as he went to a chest to take out his own pair of churidar and a loose fitting kurta.

He picked up his own sack, pulled open the door, and we stepped out onto the street. We paused to look at the distant Mount Vesuvius, the volcano that commanded much of the view from Pompeii. Smoke belched out darkly from the frothing caldera. All the people of this ancient city were soon to be dead and buried under fifteen feet of ash, lost for a millennium. I didn't want to be one of them, and I was sure Thomas didn't either.

Taking my hand, he led me back into the main thoroughfare of the Marcellum. Pompeians moved about as they would on any day, buying their food, arguing over the prices of silk, chasing beggars away. Several Roman gladiators milled about, freed from a day at the local Ludus. A dog padded up to Thomas and sniffed him. The pooch smelled the O'rmis coursing through his veins.

We headed down the avenue flanked with majestic columns, bright banners, and statues of the Roman gods. The smell of baking bread reminded me that my stomach was empty again. I thought of the fellow who ate the car. The 21st century was certainly a disaster by any standard, and an obvious success as far as Michael was concerned, but I wanted nothing more than to go home to it again. I missed my family.

Thomas and I had almost made it to the edge of the Marcellum when the very same unit of *cohortes urbanae* noticed me. They rushed us, barking orders in Latin, which could only have meant, *"Stop, or I'll shoot!"*

As they say, timing is everything. At that very moment, the ground shook violently. The columns swayed and pieces of the covered marketplace crumbled, crushing a woman who pulled a recalcitrant goat by a rope. Screams punctuated the sunny morning. People dashed by us, but the stupid Pompeian police were ever diligent in the pursuit of whom they assumed were criminals. They came toward us, despite the tremors rippling the road. Thomas dropped his sack as the leader of the stupidity squad approached. He grabbed the man and with a tremendous surge of strength, wiped the pavement with the guy. The soldier's short sword clattered toward me. I grabbed it and slashed at the incoming sentry, catching him in the thigh to open up a fountain of blood when I obviously hit the femoral artery. He went down, screeching. Thomas kicked an oncoming warrior and cold-cocked him as he swung around.

Suddenly, it became eerily quiet while we battled. It may have been only in my ears but everything sounded far away, until a minute later, the deafening blast of the erupting volcano cleared my hearing. The noise was horrendous, unspeakable, a sound that bespoke of the end of the world. Fire and rock exploded from Vesuvius. The force was so intense that pumice rained down over the city almost immediately.

People ran for their lives. We tried to follow, but apparently Roman legionnaires had a one brain cell and could only concentrate on a single thing. One of them advanced on us. I screamed for Thomas to watch out, but it was too late. The soldier got in under his defenses and plunged his sword straight into Thomas's heart. Anguish and agony crossed his face, yet he uttered not a word. He collapsed where he stood.

Time seemed to stand still. Ash swirled in the air and with each new pounding of the mountain, more pumice rained down on Pompeii. I backed up, still going one on one with two of the *cohortes*, praying that the first law of thermodynamics, that law of physics, which stated that energy could be transformed, but it could not be created or destroyed, would kick in. And then it did.

Thomas's crumbled form flared into white-hot flames. The soldiers stopped in mid-battle and mid-volcanic disaster to stare at the bonfire that was once my friend. Seconds passed. The flames abruptly fumed out and all that was left was a large pile of black ash. One of the Roman Neanderthals bellowed,

"*Lamia!*" I knew that word. It meant witch. They backed off slightly, momentarily confused by the abruptness of this funeral pyre. I advanced on the ash that was now tainted by the expulsion of the volcano. The cops leaned over it as well and that's when I saw it. The worms of solidity beginning to wiggle, the coalescence of flesh—an eye, a finger, an arm—until Thomas arose whole again, naked, his glorious gray wings fully extended, exactly like the phoenix I had tattooed on his back.

The soldiers stood transfixed, unable to move from the incredulity of the Angel's appearance. Thomas pulled me into a tight embrace. With that, the O'rmis now flowing in his body allowed him to access the folds of time and space, and once again, travel inter-dimensionally. The soldiers finally found their voices and their legs and dashed off, leaving their fallen comrades to die bloody in the street. The chaos and devastation around us shimmered, the light wavering until it finally winked out. I closed my eyes, holding onto the Angel of the Word. When I again opened them, we stood beneath a highway overpass with the sounds of rush hour to greet us.

I was home.

Timeless

Author Bios

Morgan Ashe — Morgan decided long ago that her version of reality was much better than actual reality. As such everything you read in her stories is true in her plane of existence. Sometimes, she lets her friends and family in for a peek and sometimes, she lets them leave and return to their own plane. However, if you hear a lot of screams and cries for help, just ignore them...it's only a rousing game of Parcheesi...honest.

Bob Nailor — Bob, author of the Celtic fantasy *Three Steps: The Journeys of Ayrold* and Mayan time bomb *2012: Timeline Apocalypse* resides on a quaint country acre in NW Ohio with his wife, Violet. When not in the RV traveling the country and researching his latest project, he spends his time writing, editing gardening, or spoiling his grandchildren. He is a 2008 Eppie Award winner, a contributing author to 10 anthologies and is in several more being released soon. Visit him at www.bobnailor.com for more information.

E.M. Shelton — E.M. has many skills. She is a master procrastinator, which is both useful and necessary for proper time management. She communes with the various odd creatures she seems to collect as pets (which currently include a hedgehog, a ferret, and a roommate). Arguments are a specialty of hers, and while some may choose to call her by other names, she prefers the title of debater. If you would like to debate with E.M. (or perhaps call her by some of the aforementioned names) email her at evashelton@emshelton.com

Matthew Borgard — Matthew is a software engineer living in Austin, TX with 1 cat and 1 wife. He's been writing his whole life, and is still not entirely convinced that the writers of *The Nightmare before Christmas* didn't steal the film's plot from his elementary school notebooks. He enjoys reading, writing, and partaking in video games, and does not enjoy that it is becoming increasingly difficult to do all three simultaneously. He has been published in the worlds of academia and journalism, but is a newcomer to fiction.

Kimberlie Orr — Kimberlie loves anything even remotely British. Stone circles, invading Parliamentarian soldiers, and scruffy rock bands with indecipherable English accents have all played a part in her fiction. When she's not traveling to the U.K., thinking about traveling to the U.K., or walking her fluffy black dog around historic Alexandria,

Virginia, she reads, writes, and spends way too much time on Facebook. Feel free to drop her a line via email at kimberlieorr@gmail.com.

Aaron K. Brookes—Aaron was dropped off on the steps of a haunted orphanage when he was only a few days old. His parents must not have realized that the orphanage was no longer operational, but luckily the ghosts took him in. The building that the orphanage had been in was once a boarding house for failed writers, and it is their ghosts who now haunt the location. They taught him everything he knows.

Elyse Salpeter — Elyse is the author of five novels, including her young adult thriller FLYING TO THE LIGHT, recently published by Cool Well Press. Her short stories have appeared in a host of magazines and anthologies, such as *Beyond Centauri, Tales of the Talisman, Fifty Something Magazine* and *Nights of Blood 2*. A mom of ten year old twins, she spends her time working in ad sales during the day, cooking gourmet meals for her family, going to Tae Kwon Do, and squeezing in any free moment to work on her newest writing project.

Ann Swann — Someone dreamed Ann into existence one warm summer eve when it was said the immortals first floated to Earth in their shimmering orbs. Perhaps that coincidence is what possessed Ann to begin recording the machinations of those ethereal creatures. She hopes it brings her closer to her elusive creator. It has occurred to Ann that she may simply be a character in one of her own tales. Stranger things have happened. If you would like to discuss creation myths with Ann, or perhaps read more of her musings disguised as fiction, email her at swannann76@yahoo.com or visit AnnSwann.blogspot.com

Denise Vitola—Denise is the author of numerous science fiction novels and short stories, but her special claim to fame is her ability to bi-locate, or in layman's terms, to be in two and a half places at once. She regularly appears at her authors' favorite writing cafes to badger them about missing deadlines and not hitting word counts. While being seen at these trendy spots and spilling espresso down her shirt, she is always instantly available to answer silly questions at the Cool Well Press offices as she edits manuscripts and eats chocolate cake. And while she's doing all that, part of her is dilly-dallying on Shadow Street, trying to find the perfect Goth yarn shop. But she always welcomes email from fans, so drop her a line at editor@coolwellpress.com. Once she's done knitting the scarf for the company hellhound, she'll get back to you.